tales for
EXPECTANT
FATHERS

William Van Wert

tales for
EXPECTANT
FATHERS

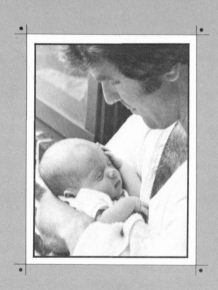

THE DIAL PRESS
New York

for Ian, who keeps me expectant

Published by
The Dial Press
1 Dag Hammarskjold Plaza
New York, New York 10017

"Krishna's Flute" first appeared in *Ascent;* "Lie Still" first appeared in *Cottonwood Review;* "The Ninth Month" first appeared in *Northwest Review*. The Publisher is grateful for permission to print the stories here.

The photographs on pages 37 and 85 are used by permission of David R. Godine Publisher, Inc.

The photograph on page 23 is used courtesy of James W. Fitzgerald.

All other photographs are used by permission of Aina Balgalvis.

Library of Congress Cataloging in Publication Data

Van Wert, William F.
Tales for expectant fathers.

Contents: Krishna's flute — Dolls — The woman at the well — [etc.]
  I. Title.
PS3572.A417T3 1982   813'.54   82.9636
ISBN 0-385-27798-9

Contents

Krishna's Flute

I teach film courses at a large metropolitan university. I feared the coming of June and the end of classes, because it left me with nothing to do but twiddle my thumbs and wait out the last month or so of my wife's pregnancy. I tried to read the books on childbirth. I tried to keep a diary. I tried to make lists of things to buy and things to do for the birth. Mostly I gave my wife added indigestion and anxiety. Reluctantly she agreed to my plan to teach a film course to the eight-to-ten age bracket at the Allen Lane Art Center Summer Camp. All of these facts are interconnected.

My film course might not have been possible had there not been a heated debate between the male and female staff members at the center already raging over the merits and demerits of purchasing enormous amounts of sports equipment, from tennis rackets and baseball gloves to Frisbees and miniature barbells. The men were all for buying the equipment. Sports would get the kids outdoors and complement the indoors arts-and-crafts classes like painting, ceramics, and dance. They argued that the boys would be able to excel in outdoor sports and thus offset the girls excelling in the indoors arts and crafts. The women were against all the sports equipment. Not just because of the cost, which was high, but also because they felt that sports would encourage unhealthy competition in the kids. Besides, they argued, the sports equipment would be of little use in the winter, and the center had no place to store it until the next summer's camp. They had reached a stalemate. So rather than either side giving in, they both compromised. They accepted my film course, which called for purchasing Kodak and Bell & Howell super-8 movie cameras, enough rental money for several short films, and enough money to pay for developing four or five three-minute films to be made by the children themselves. There were twelve kids in the class, so each film would represent the collective work of four people. So many fours on paper must have given them a sense of symmetry. Total cost: Seven hundred dollars. They scrapped their plans and economized on the sports equipment. They bought Frisbees, jump ropes, and Hula-Hoops. They accepted my course. I have not altered any of the facts.

I arrived for the first day of class. Where twelve eager faces should have been, there was only a gaunt man in a tie-dyed shirt, blue jeans with American flags on the back pockets, sandals with frayed straps. He looked up at me. His beard was full of red baby curls. His wild blue eyes bulged behind horn-rim glasses. He sniffed a couple times, the symptom no doubt of a summer cold or the telltale sign of a cocaine afficionado.

"Hey, man, what's happenin'?"

"I'm not sure. I was supposed to find twelve kids here."

"You the film teacher?"

"Yes I am. My name's Keith Hammond. What's yours?"

He smiled at my extended hand, did not raise his own, smiled at my face with his face still scrunched.

"Hurley. Just plain Hurley, man. You're gonna find out the boy brats here insist on last names. For them and for the staff, same thing. The little ladies, well, they like first names. They blush when you call their first names. They giggle when they call you by your first name. I piss 'em off and call 'em by their last names. Been doing this every summer for six years. They still don't know my first name."

I noticed for the first time that his left cheek bulged in a ball. Chewing tobacco, I surmised. My hand was still there, extended.

"Hey, man, sorry about shaking hands. Can't do it, though. Got a bad index here."

He held up the index finger of his right hand. It was purple but not swollen. Obviously dead. I would learn much later that Hurley had avoided the draft by killing that index finger. He made a practice of sticking it into burning pipe bowls, gradually singeing the nerve endings and killing all feeling. He couldn't bend the finger finally and so could never be counted on to pull the trigger in any war.

"I'm a carpenter by shtick"—he thumbed the hammer that hung by his belt loop on the right side of his pants—"but I do ceramics with the natives."

"I see. I'm glad to meet you and talk to you, but I'm a little worried about being late for my class."

"Wrong room. They're down the hall, last one on the right. Don't sweat it. By the time you're through with 'em, you'll want to keep the little bastards waiting. Drive you to crabs, you'll see."

I tried to smile. I was already backpedaling my way out of the room and down the hall.

"Say, Hammond, what do you think of Jap films?"

"I don't understand."

"You know, Kurosawa and them cats. I mean, slow as Moses up the mount. They just keep pulling the trigger, you dig, I mean they must tie their fingers to the thing."

I was still trying to smile. I had never thought about Japanese films that way before. I wondered if I could think up something to say about clay drinking mugs before the summer was over.

I walked into my classroom, a room whose original architect must have been shorter than the children who awaited me. Mobiles hung everywhere from the low ceiling. Crayon graffiti and stick-face drawings peppered the walls. I remembered having seen such walls once in a *Psy-*

chology Today photo, illustrating the therapy techniques of R. D. Laing. The linoleum floor was divided into yellow and orange squares. In every yellow square was the face of the sun, smiling. Three of the eight boys were chasing one of the four girls, shouting, "Pussy, tease," in repeated refrains. Two of the remaining boys were trying to drown a bug they had just wounded with their spit. And the shortest of the remaining boys sat by himself in the last desk of the last row nearest the window. He was lighting matches. I called them to order and read off the names: Marshall Chrisler, Kathleen Duggan, Saralee Epstein, Winston Feeney . . . on down to Margaret Zimmerman.

"Look, if it's okay with you people, I'd like you to call me Keith. And I'd like to call you all by your first names . . ."

There were scowls among the boys.

". . . or all by your last names."

Now the girls were frowning, especially Saralee Epstein. Feeney suggested we put it to a vote. Without thinking, I agreed. Of course the boys prevailed, and it was last names. They also voted that I would be just plain Hammond, not Mr. Hammond.

". . . as in organ?"

It was Lieberman who said this, and everyone else sniggled (a cross between giggling and salivating). Lieberman stared evenly at me, no emotion at all on his acne-festered face. I explained that Annie and I were expecting a baby, that I had never taught children before, that I hoped to learn a lot from them.

"Margaret can teach you all you want about babies, Ham."

"Andy Lieberman, you piece of horseshit—"

"Okay, okay. That's enough, both of you. I just wanted to let you know, that's all. It's not important anyway. Now let's—"

"You gonna film it?"

"I don't know. I mean, we haven't decided. At least, I don't think so. You kids probably don't know yet how these things work, but everything happens very fast. I mean, I'll be very busy."

I was stumbling, losing control in the first five minutes. Everyone looked approvingly at Feeney for the power his question had had over me, everyone except Lieberman, who would have bit Feeney's lower lip, if looks were snakes.

I began to explain the organization of the course. I was interrupted again.

"Hey, Hammond, this is day camp, not school. Are you thinking of giving us grades or something?"

It was Chrisler, who had led the three-way charge on Saralee Epstein when I first entered the room. I explained that grades would not be given, but that I would write up their individual performances for their parents at the end of camp. I explained that I hoped the class would be fun for everyone. I tried to find out what were their favorite films.

"*The Wild Bunch,*" said Chrisler.

"*Bad News Bears,*" said Kathleen Duggan.

"I don't know," said Saralee Epstein, just to say something.

"*The Seven Samurai,*" offered Feeney, after everyone else had spoken.

"You mean *The Magnificent Seven,* don't you, Feeney? *The Seven Samurai* is a Japanese film."

Feeney wasn't speaking.

"Do you really mean *The Seven Samurai*? How did you see it?"

"Hurley, the clay teacher, took me. He's in the neighborhood. Takes us to lots of them films."

I expected to see a miniature hammer hanging by Feeney's belt loop, but there wasn't any. This kind of exploratory questioning worked fine with college students. Why wasn't it working with these kids? Already I was losing their attention. Soon they would be outdoors with Frisbees and jump ropes. I had to make some kind of impression. I brought out the cameras.

The cameras were all either Kodak or Bell & Howell super-8. I showed them a piece of regular-8 film and compared it with a strip of super-8. I told them about the sprocket holes and how sound was added to the film. I showed them how to load the cartridge film. They crowded around me, the girls to my left, the boys in front and to my right. I explained that the Fotomat down the street had agreed to develop our films with a waiting period of just two days for each. We would shoot our films at the beginning of the week, we would watch rented films in the middle of the week, and we would view and critique the student films at the end of the week.

"What do you mean, 'critique'?"

"Just a term, Chrisler. We'll comment on each other's films, that's all."

"You gonna make films with us, Hammond? I think you should have to make 'em if you're gonna say anything about ours. How's that? You gonna make 'em too, Hammond?"

"We'll see, Chrisler, we'll see."

"How was it?" Annie asked, still half asleep from her afternoon nap.

"Medium cool," I joked, and nobody laughed. I forgot to ask her how her day had been.

Hurley was waiting for me the next day when I walked in.

"Hey, man, one of my main men tells me you're some kind of heavy."

"What's that mean?"

"Means you got some notion that these little hollowweenies are supposed to learn something. I mean, man, that's radical, ain't so?"

"Who's your informer? Feeney?"

"I never lie, man. Yep, it was the Feen all right.

He's in there today. You should be flattered, Hammond."

"Why?"

" 'Cause that little bugger is a chronic, that's why. I mean, last summer he must have showed all of one third of the days. A different illness every day. Even told me one day that his wisdom teeth were bothering him. But he told me he guessed he wouldn't miss as much this summer. Can't wait to pull that trigger, I guess."

"Well, thanks for the information, Hurley. I'll see you later."

"Wait a minute, man. Wanted to ask you if you wanted to go to the flicks with us tonight. There's a Bruce Lee triple-header at the Grove. Tremendous special effects, man. Want to go?"

"Not tonight, Hurley. Some other time, huh?"

I gave the class their first assignment. They were to break up into teams, go outdoors, and in their three-minute films film each member of the group in the act of doing something right there on the grounds. If the films were good enough, I joked, we might show them to the rest of the camp.

"Are you going to watch us while we film?" asked Annette Kupchak.

"No, I'll stay inside today."

"Fat job, Mr. Hammond," chimed Lieberman in his most cherubic tones.

"Can we film anything we want to?" asked Feeney, leadingly.

"Anything."

Annie was awake and waiting to talk when I got home. She wanted to talk about our upcoming home birth. She hadn't talked to anyone all day. I hadn't either, with the exception of Hurley and the few questions asked at class. Still, I didn't feel like talking. Annie felt like getting up, like going out, to a movie maybe. I didn't feel like a movie. I felt like lying still, my eyes open in the dark of our bedroom, my hand on her pregnant stomach next to me. She didn't feel like lying down, since she had already had two naps that day. So we compromised, as often we do, and watched television, a movie on television. It was one of those cleaned-up westerns, in which one of the main subthemes was the separation and eventual reunion of a mother horse with her baby colt. Annie didn't stay around for the reunion, made possible by a little Mexican boy named Pablo. She went to bed crying for the lost baby colt.

The next day was Thursday. My legs hurt for some reason as I walked up to the center. I felt bowlegged. The class had a similar feel to it, a little blurred, a little bowed, like watching it from a fish-eye lens. We watched two Chaplin films. I had hoped to show them how exaggerated gestures and facial types could create comedy by contrast. It was bowlegged Charlie with his bowler hat and cane versus Edna Purviance with her wet full lips and the halo lighting around her hair, and the two of them versus Eric Campbell, the bully, with his close-shaven head, his painted-on eyebrows, his fat belly protruding from the too-tight vest. It worked with college students. Why didn't it work with these children? Obviously, I asked.

"If Charlie had talked with a harelip . . ." Lieberman, of course.

"If the lady weren't so sweet and if she turned out to be the bully and beat up Charlie and the bully . . ." Margaret Zimmerman.

"If they hadn't been so mushy with their eyebrows . . ." Chrisler.

"If Charlie's hat wasn't a hat but a grenade in disguise and if his cane weren't a cane at all but a samurai sword in disguise . . ." Who else? Feeney.

I asked them if, maybe, it wasn't too funny for them because it was old. If I had used Spanky and Our Gang or The Three Stooges. No, they all said, that wouldn't have helped. But Mary Tyler Moore and Archie Bunker were definitely funnier. I went home and watched *All in the Family* that night. The show was about abortion. How could my class find it funny? I thought. How could they even understand it? And what happened, between their age and the age of my college students, to make Charlie Chaplin funny again?

Before the Friday class I picked up the finished films at the Fotomat.

"Lots of home movies here, huh, fella?" winked and cajoled the Fotomat man behind his tiger-striped Formica counter.

"Hey, Hammond, I hear it's Oscar day in the outer banks," shuffled Hurley from behind his whirling wheel of captive pots, and it seemed like his smile was too toothy for a Friday. And too caked with clay.

I remember setting up the projector and screen. I remember threading some of the films. I wish I had kept a diary at the time, to verify my stupor at some of the things I saw. Epstein had filmed Chrisler at the drinking fountain, had filmed him in medium shot, then to a close-up of Chrisler's open mouth, not really drinking, just driveling water. There was laughter and applause everywhere. Hurley popped his head around the door and asked if the films were X-rated, leaving before I could give any answer. Whoever filmed the next segment had figured out the zoom. A long shot of Epstein holding a Hula-Hoop went to a close-up of the Hula-Hoop, then in and out, from close-up to long shot of the hole in the Hula-Hoop.

"Andy Lieberman, you filthy piece of horseshit."

Margaret Zimmerman had a limited vocabulary, I decided. The next segment showed Epstein fingering her braces.

"You liar. You said you weren't filming them." It was Epstein in the dark, accusing without naming the accused. But in the dark her accusation was amplified, the crime more grievous, and so I didn't ask who had been behind the camera. The last segment, just before the film ran out, showed a smiling Lieberman urinating on the azaleas. I asked who had filmed that segment, shifting the responsibility for Lieberman's lewdness to the person who had captured that act for posterity. It was time for Zimmerman to deliver. She said nothing. I wondered.

Another film showed a close-up of one of Hurley's pots and then a close-up of one of Hurley's eyeballs. In the first close-up it was Hurley's hands that spun the pots, that made the circles go round. In the close-up of the eyeball the hands on the camera created the swirling circles. I didn't need to ask.

In another segment Duggan was jumping rope, Kupchak and Tanner holding the ends of the rope. That was innocuous enough. Mine was the only sigh in the whole room. And suddenly the camera was on the ground, filming up at what, had they been in focus, would have been Duggan's underpants. What planet is this? I could hear my mind asking as the film went flicker-flicker on the take-up reel.

I seem to remember that the last segment of the very last film was of Feeney holding a burning match. Again, a close-up. Why did these kids all decide they had to use close-ups? It was a close-up of the match burning to the fingers that held the dimming fire for a second, then moved out of focus, extinguishing the flame.

"Who was behind the camera for that one, Feeney?"

No answer. What was there to hide? Did the guilty person think I was going to report him or her to the fire department?

"Feeney?"

"Nobody."

"What do you mean, 'nobody'?"

"Nobody, that's all. I set the camera on top of the picnic bench, put it to 'time' and then ran in front of it to film myself. Too bad it didn't work."

"I don't understand. Of course it worked, and it

was very ingenious of you, Feeney, to have figured that out by yourself."

"I don't mean that. I wanted the match to burn the film at the end, to get inside the camera and burn the end of the film, so's everybody would see the film burn just like the match burned."

Now that was a response that really should have been reported to the fire department. How much insurance did Feeney's neighbors have on their houses? I would have to ask Hurley, I thought.

"Okay, very interesting films. Very interesting. Not exactly what I would have expected. Any comments?"

No comments. Of course there were no comments. There were only giggles and hands clapping in applause. So this was comedy for them. Archie Bunker was as docile as Rin Tin Tin compared to this. I should have been a psychologist, I thought, not a film teacher. I was certainly not equipped to deal with this class-wide narcissus complex.

The weekend brought relief, except for those moments when Annie regressed to her three-year-old state, curling up in a fetal ball and asking me to touch her toes. I turned off the television every time a child appeared on screen. I began to wonder if our still unborn baby was dreaming of matches in Annie's womb. I would never again complain about teaching apathetic college students. I never thought I would come to appreciate their creased smiles and lusterless, sandblasted eyes. Hurley had no monopoly on clay.

Monday came and I crawled out of bed like a bruised quarterback after a Sunday game. The analogy seemed appropriate to me, since it was me and my cameras who had spared the children their sore shoulders from football pads, their bruised knees from sliding into second base, their tennis elbows and soccer black eyes. Somehow I didn't feel like Florence Nightingale for sparing them this pain.

The second week's assignment was portrait work,

each student taking turns posing for a portrait, handling the crude lighting for someone else's portrait, handling the camera for yet another portrait. Three-minute film after three-minute film of staged faces, exaggerated eyebrows and lipstick on both the girls and boys. In my more innocent moments I really believed they had learned the lesson of caricature in Chaplin's films. In my deeper, more frequent suspicions, however, I wondered if I weren't sending them down the road to transvestism.

"Want to take my picture, big boy?"

I didn't even notice at the time that Hurley was wearing lipstick when he asked me this. I didn't remember what I had seen until I got home and saw the sweat on Annie's forehead, the parched lips open like the green on a desert golf course.

"Are you all right, Annie?"

"Better now. I wish you had been here two hours ago."

What was I doing, after all, spending the last precious moments of the pregnancy teaching films to miniature grown-ups in order to learn what it would be like to be around children? Why couldn't I have learned by staying at home, by watching ashtrays move on Annie's stomach, by putting my ears to her belly and hearing the hiccoughs and groans of our as yet uncoddled toddler? It was a little like going to Vietnam to teach in order not to go there as a soldier. I had done that too.

I showed my class *The Red Balloon, The Magician,* and a couple other antiwar films for children in the third week. They found these films to be "funny in the focus," "silly," and "weird, man." Or was it Hurley who added the last? Their own film assignment for the week was to make a film on the center grounds that had a social message, that made some kind of moral statement. So what did we get on Friday? You can't waterski on summer grass, said one film loud and clear. Garbage smells good once you get used to it, said another. Matches burn brighter than flashlights during the day, said another. How would presidential hopefuls appeal to this crowd once it reached voting age? I thought in despair.

"Got some kinky little triggers in there, don't you?"

"I'm sorry, Hurley. I didn't hear what you said."

"It's okay, man. Say, you seem a little spaced lately. Is your lady's due date coming up?"

"How did you know that?"

"The Feen, man."

It was true. I was distracted. The birth was soon, very soon, the first week in July, said the doctor. Better than August, I thought. I couldn't afford to buy an air conditioner just to keep Annie cool.

I have even less recollection of the following week. Their film assignment was to create a story, to write it together, to act it out and film it. I remember that Lieberman pulled Zimmerman's hair and Zimmerman responded by kneeing Lieberman in the groin in one of the films. It was clear to me and everyone else there that these two hostile acts had not been scripted in the film. In the film that Feeney "directed," there was a cut from Chrisler and Duggan holding hands to a close-up of the red fire-alarm box and back to the hands being held. I don't remember anything else. There's been a birth between then and now.

I do remember assigning the final film project early, so that they would have time to think about it and work on it. For the first time they would be able to check the cameras out, take them home, and film away from the center. They were to film a story again, this time of their own choosing. I suggested that their films should in some way reflect their home lives. Feeney waited for me in the hall after class.

"I was thinking . . . well, I guess it's weird . . . well . . ."

"Feeney. What's up? Just spit it out. It's not like you to stumble around."

"Okay, here it is. I want to film your wife's baby being born, that's all."

I did one of those Did-I-hear-you-say-what-I-think-I-heard-you-say double takes. I felt insulted in the belly, the proxy for my Annie's belly's privacy having been invaded, as though my swan dive had just turned to a belly-smacker.

"You're kidding."

No answer. I thought about Feeney invisible behind the camera filming a visible Feeney holding a burning match. I had visions of a personless camera at our birth and Feeney coming out of Annie's last pushing.

"Feeney, say you're kidding."

No answer.

"Feeney, I don't think you understood me in there. I want you all to go home and film your own families, to film something that will reflect your own home life. Okay?"

He left without a word of rebuttal, his head down, his hands in his pockets.

"He wasn't kidding," said an eavesdropping Hurley, for the first time serious and soberly un-hip with me. Before I could explain, he too had turned and closed off discussion.

"But it's preposterous, Annie. I only told you because I thought you'd laugh. I never thought you'd take it seriously."

"I think it's sweet."

"But the kid's a pyromaniac, I tell you. He'd o.d. on all the candles you want lit around the bed."

"You've talked about him before. Feeney, right? You've told me each Friday when you came home that he was original, that he had promise, that he was sensitive."

"Maybe so, but this is different. I mean, that's class and this is home."

"That doesn't seem very reasonable to me. Look, you want to have the birth filmed. You know you'll be a nervous wreck working with me. You know you could never distance yourself enough to do the film yourself."

"But he's just a kid . . ."

"The midwife's daughter will be there. She's younger than this Feeney."

"I know, but he's at a more impressionable age. I mean, all the blood and seeing you naked and all. . . ."

"Are you speaking for yourself or for Feeney? This Hurley told you that Feeney had no family life to speak of that he could film. He told you Feeney's mother was dead and that his father traveled a lot, and that this summer camp was a good way to keep Feeney out of trouble while his father traveled."

"So that was according to Hurley. What does he know?"

As it turned out, he knew a lot. I just didn't want to admit that a washed-out hippie with red baby curls for a beard and an obnoxious hammer hanging by his belt loop and a clay handshake that threatened to turn you into a statue could know more than a college film teacher or hyperexpectant father.

I couldn't tell him to his face, so I telephoned. Feeney's aunt said that whatever was okay for me was okay for Winston. She was glad to help. Where was Feeney? Off to the movies, of course.

So when the time came for final class presentations, only Feeney was filmless, waiting as I was for Annie to give the word. The films were surprisingly touching and sensitive. Saralee Epstein reunited her divorced parents for an interview, with many close-ups of the nervous rubbing of their hands, which she taped on cassette. They were visibly embarrassed by the film, and Mr. Epstein mentioned that he would certainly speak to Saralee's teacher when the class was over. Chrisler did a film composed entirely of pan shots of his father's tax-law books, shelves and shelves of dust-covered books. Lieberman chronicled the deaths of his pet goldfish. Duggan contrasted her little sister's room, filled with stuffed animals and Dr. Seuss books, with her own, which was neater, more somber, now filled with posters of the latest rock groups. I believe that every one of these films had at least ten seconds in them that were highly professional. I never did understand why these children were so obsessed with close-ups, but I could see that they were gradually using these close-ups for good reasons. I can take no credit for the sophistication that I found in these films. They had learned in spite of me.

And the last class ended without laughter or applause. A heavy kind of calm had settled in their young bodies. Their eyes were clear but colorless. Adult eyes, I thought. Maybe they could laugh at Chaplin now, I thought. And to my surprise Lieberman was carrying Zimmerman's bookbag when the two left the room. Only Feeney still seemed the child to me. I told him I would call him when Annie was ready to deliver.

"See you next week, Hammond?"

"What's next week, Hurley?"

"Meeting with the parents. You get to see the faces behind these little devils."

"Okay. See you then."

"Hey, man . . ."

"Yes?"

"Good luck on your own little devil."

I would have forgotten to call him. I was so wrapped up in fetching orange-juice ice cubes, in swabbing Annie's sweaty forehead, in coaching her on her breathing. For some reason she remembered. With her eyes closed between two of the heaviest and longest contractions, half out of her head, she remembered.

"Call Feeney."

"What?"

"It's time to call Feeney. You promised."

I called Feeney. He sounded less excited than I had anticipated over the telephone. He said he would be right over, but he said it in a monotone. I didn't understand why, until I had hung up. It was the evening of July Fourth, and I could hear explosions in the distance. Poor

Feeney. He would be giving up the biggest bonfire of the year, giving up firecrackers, sparklers, cherry bombs, and the aerial fireworks show downtown to come and film a baby being born. I felt sorry for him. At his age I would have chosen the firecrackers.

"Are you ready?"

"Yes, sir."

He had never called me "sir" before. What made him more formal in the privacy of our bedroom than he had been for weeks in the open spaces of the art center? I didn't have time to figure it out. I only know that Annie remembered to smile at him once or twice between contractions. I remember that it must have been difficult for him, waiting three hours for the three minutes of film he would take of the baby's head coming out. At least a close-up would certainly not be out of place here. I don't know whether I just trusted Feeney, and so ignored him, or whether I didn't trust my own emotions, and so plunged my attention even deeper into the screams of Annie and the excited whispers of the midwife.

"It's coming. One more push, Annie. One more."

I cannot describe the process of that moment, the millions of fears and delights a man and woman go through in that one last push. I can only describe the end result. A syrupy head went *whoosh* and blew into the waiting hands of the midwife. Its face was a little squashed and contorted, a little wrinkled like Mr. Magoo, a little wizened and aged with the trip through the tubes. It was a boy. It could have been a girl, and we would have been happy. It could have been a frog at that point, as long as it came out.

I don't know when it happened. In the excitement no one else had noticed either. But there was Feeney, the camera on his lap, eyes closed in the chair near the bed. Had he fainted or just fallen asleep? Annie laughed.

"It takes a lot to be a wise man on Christmas Eve."

I didn't exactly understand Annie's remark or why she said it. She had never been a particularly religious person. She held our baby on her chest, between her breasts. She rubbed his little buttocks gently up and down with instinctive fingers. She told me to hold Feeney the way she was holding our baby. For some reason I was more worried about holding the camera than I was about holding Feeney.

"Did it happen?"

"Yes, Feeney. It was a boy."

"I don't know what happened. I was filming and the last thing I remember, there was this firecracker went off about two blocks away."

"It's okay, Feeney. I'll get developed what you did film and tell you how it came out."

"You're sure lucky, Mr. Hammond."

"Oh, you mean the baby. Thank you, Feeney."

"No, I mean your wife. She's very pretty without her clothes on."

For some reason the pregnancy would not be over for me until I had seen that film. It was as if some proof were needed, Feeney's proof, that we had really had our baby before I could fully believe. I shouldn't have been surprised by what came out in that film. I really shouldn't, since Feeney had always filmed the unexpected. Still, I was surprised. Feeney's film began with the candle burning beside our bed. It began with a close-up of one of Annie's yoga books lying next to the candle. It went to her eyes and on down her body, stopping at the heaving belly, the belly pumping in contractions, the belly flaccid and full like a hidden basketball that no one was dribbling. It lingered on that belly and would not go lower, even though the life inside had already descended. Instead, it went up, not back to Annie's face, but to mine, up to my eyes and the tears and sweat inside my eyes. It hung on my eyes, it jarred, and then it ended, abruptly, with the candle and yoga book out of focus behind my head. I was disappointed that there had been no record of our baby Brian's head crowning and coming through.

But Annie was happy. And Feeney was pleased with his film.

"It didn't freeze at the end is all. I wanted to film that blue, you know? There was more blueness than people. I wanted to freeze it all, to put the whole film in an ice cube. You'd have to thaw it out to see it, and then all that blue would go zing to orange and red and yellow. You know what I mean, Mr. Hammond?"

"I guess so, Feeney. By the way, I think you can call me Keith."

"Well, okay. But don't you call me Winston. I hate that name."

It should have ended with the last class, but it didn't. It should have ended with the filming of the birth, but it didn't. And it didn't really end with meeting the parents that second week in July. Saralee Epstein's parents were there. Separately they sought me out and asked me the exact same questions with exactly the same words and intonation. Who did I think I was, anyway, trying to tamper with something as sacred as their divorce? Lieberman's mother complained that she was going broke paying for Lieberman's two films a week. She complained, but she was smiling. Margaret Zimmerman's father asked me in a whisper if I thought it was time to tell her the facts of life. How did I know? Watch her films and decide, I told him. And Feeney's aunt was there, a shriveled-up woman. She was forty, she said, but she looked eighty-three. She didn't even mention the class. She told me that Feeney's mother had died in childbirth, delivering Feeney. She told me that she didn't want to be melodramatic, but she thought Feeney's father had never quite forgiven Feeney for that death. There was no connection, of course, but suddenly I understood why a boy would film himself getting burned by a match.

It could have ended there. The class was over. Annie was thin again. Brian was sucking fifty times a day like a barracuda at her breasts. And I would soon begin fall classes. It could have ended there, but it didn't. I had fathered two sons over the summer, one by blood and one by fire. I began going to the movies every Friday night with Feeney and Hurley. Even Hurley got to calling me Keith, and he seemed happy to share Feeney with me. He even left his hammer at home.

Dolls

*D*OLLS. It began with dolls. Will end with dolls. In my father's day dolls used to be leggy women in purple or pink high heels with a lot of cheek between the eyebrows and the kneecaps, not the wooden, wide-eyed stuffies that kids play with. Not those Raggedy Anns with hair like orange spaghetti that cats rip and gnarl to bits. Not the bionic amazons with flashlight batteries for eyeballs and the swivel elbows that make construction workers envious. Dolls.

I became obsessed with dolls when Shirley got pregnant. Some men get involved with antique cars, with making little wooden rocking chairs, with buying telescopes and staying up all night staring at the stars. Some men get into other women. Me, I became a doll junkie. I will never believe that the kid that comes out of Shirley isn't really a doll in disguise. Since the third month of the pregnancy Shirley has gone inward on me. Her motions are mechanical; her speech seems controlled by some electronic trigger behind the bloodshot eyes. I suspect that Shirley is not a woman after all. She is Mattel's most perfect answer to prepartum depression.

I sit here eating cold chicken soup. It's supposed to be good for fevers, and Shirley has a fever. But Shirley wasn't hungry, and my mother always told me to eat what was on my plate, even if the plate wasn't mine. All those starving dolls in India, you know.

I sit here thinking that women's liberation has made it possible for women to contemplate pregnancy without simultaneously contemplating suicide. I mean, it must be a comfort to Shirley to know that I sit here eating chicken soup, because she is my equal. And because she is my equal, I think I am starting a fever. But then they make dolls nowadays that sweat real sweat beads (Mattel set up a special contract with Morton to put real salt in those sweat beads), so who can tell? Someone may just be pulling my string is all.

I sit here thinking that women's liberation has allowed both men and women to go out and work three quarters of their lives. They have the same chances for strokes, heart attacks, ulcers, pneumonia. Pneumonia? What am I saying? Unless, of course, you're a door-to-door underwear salesperson in Greenland. I must be starting a fever.

They now have the same chances of being away from home and, more to my point, away from children, who are really smart these days. They raise themselves at home. There's a lot of talk about the effect of television on children, but most of the talk is published in *TV Guide,* so you can never tell. Me, I think the real parents of today's children are the dolls they keep. You can tell a person by the doll company he/she keeps. These dolls aren't just idle company either. They're bosom bodies, lovers, companions, parents to the kids. And they teach children death. The first time Baby Tender Love does its patented (U.S., that is) sneeze and nothing but hot air comes out, the kid knows what terminal leukemia is. And how about Willie Wetdream? I mean, you're supposed to twist the little bugger's arm and watch his trousers get bigger, until the Mississippi goes peepee in his pants. And when the drains get clogged and the little harmless liquid accumulates some mucous in the membranes, well, kids are bound to get an idea of what herpes is.

I've forgotten that Shirley and I have already decided on a name for our baby, whatever its sex. I've forgotten what those names were. No matter how hard I try to remember, I keep coming up Ken and Barbie. I will probably have to ask Shirley what those names were after the birth. Shirley worries a lot about our baby's health. She says I shouldn't smoke, because our baby might inhale the smoke through Shirley's pores. She worries about the baby's birthmarks. She prays that they won't appear on the tip of its nose. A couple on its tush would be okay. She thinks birthmarks may be floating around in there, and every time the baby does a somersault inside, it may be transferring those marks from its buttocks to the tip of its nose. Shirley worries about how fragile young babies are. Me, I spend most of my time away from the house in the company of dime-store dolls, so I don't worry as much. I expect our baby to be highly breakable.

Jumpsie jumps rope and never misses. I think about counting sheep in the dreams of my childhood, and I pray to God that Jumpsie might miss just one time and bang his little shins. And bleed real blood, so Shirley and I can be useful as parents and put maple syrup or butter or turpentine on the wound and kiss the booboos away.

The white version of Talking Drowsy says: "Mommy, kiss me and good night." I can see Shirley now, reduced to her knees like an automaton, obeying, wishing secretly that just once T.D. would ask for a bedtime story. I can see the whole routine having a boomerang effect on our marriage. No long talks until three in the A. M., like we used to, no mad scramble of tongues and thighs (Shirley calls it "snow flurries and thundershowers") like we used to. Just "kiss me and good night." The black version of T.D. says: "Cool it, baby" and "Can you dig it?" Shirley and I could conceivably have a black baby, although I don't see how, unless Shirley knows more than I and isn't telling. But not even a kiss and good night. You say "go to sleep, little baby" and it calls you "baby" back. Maybe that's baby liberation.

Shirley groans from her midafternoon nap of nightmares and asks:

"Who are you talking to out there?"

"Talking Drowsy, honey."

"Me too. I feel real lousy."

I take an Excedrin time capsule. I like them, because they call them time capsules. I imagine myself on

Pluto. If I took a time capsule there, I wouldn't get instant relief on Earth until twenty years later. That's a long headache.

The time dolls march by. There's a whole series of time dolls. They're programmed with hourly commands for the kids. It's two o'clock, let's take a nap. It's seven o'clock, let's brush our teeth. Only at one o'clock do the dolls falter. At one o'clock they ask: "What do we do now?" I once shouted a bunch of obscene instructions in the ear of one of those dolls when it asked its one o'clock question. At two o'clock it was still in a funk. You can even blow a doll's mind these days. It's probably because they're really humans in disguise. Anal retentives, at that.

Good Girl Barbie has the head of a gorgon, a Medusa whose snakes need constant combing, shampooing, styling. She requires lipstick and rouge too. I once took Good Girl Barbie out on one of those ten-day trials, money back guaranteed. I smeared her hair with lipstick and rouge. I drowned her open mouth with Head & Shoulders. At least she didn't have to worry about dandruff on her lower intestines. I took her back at the end of ten days and said I wasn't satisfied. I wonder whatever happened to Good Girl Barbie. She probably had to go to reform school.

Shirley reminds me that the telephone is ringing. I pick up the receiver and let my telephone doll do all the talking. It always talks. It's incapable of listening. It initiates stupidities like "Tell me a secret" and "Scratch my back" and "How about tea at my house today?" When I really think about the number of telephone calls I've received in my life that were of any importance at all, I feel much better about letting the telephone doll do all the talking. Besides, it's cheaper than an answering service.

As a child gets older, the dolls get more active, more aggressive, more tyrannical. They really know how to whip little kids into shape. The dolls always win in any verbal struggle, because the kids never get a chance to speak. But the dolls pretend to be subservient by doing menial tasks or by performing magic transformations. Growing Up Skipper (Gus, for short) is a limp little blond doll that zaps into puberty with a twist of her left arm. You twist the little leftie and suddenly a Raquel Welch bust starts popping the buttons off the tomboy T-shirt. As an aside, I've seen a lot of teen-age girls with their left arms in a sling lately. I always thought they were due to skiing accidents or tripping on their Frisbees or something. Then there's Tiffany Taylor, who changes hair colors. Turn her head and she's a blonde. The Japanese want to patent this doll. They really do. Just think about what the Kabuki prints of the twenty-third century will look like. Dizzy Lizzie irons and swings. I suppose she irons to teach little girls how to work when they become adults. And then she swings to teach them how to play. Ironing and swinging, ironing and swinging. No wonder the divorce rate is so high these days.

Shirley says she can't stand it anymore. She knows she's not supposed to take any aspirin, because it might turn our unborn baby into a Bufferin addict, but she can't help it. She begs me to bring her an aspirin. In the dark, I bring her some M & M's instead. She doesn't think it's very funny.

I go back to the kitchen and Nancy Nonsense is there, with her 217 different taped statements inside her little unpregnant belly. Around her neck is a tag that announces to any old emptor that there's a $1.50 rebate on Nancy. Words are indeed cheap these days.

When Shirley was a little girl growing up, there was still a thing that we nostalgically refer to as the "country." Her father had twenty acres of pine forest in southern Georgia, and Shirley grew up without any dolls. She talked to the trees; she learned to tell the difference between the fat female pine cones and the long skinny males. She had a pet horse she rode around and got thrown off of. She went fishing with her father and learned the names of a hundred flowers from her mother. Shirley has had headaches ever since we moved to the city.

"I'm going out for a little action."

I say this to Shirley and I'm purposefully evasive. I don't want her to think I'm a sure thing. I want her to imagine me carousing in some topless all-night bar or banging into the "men working in trees" signs on the city streets or whatever pregnant women think when their husbands say they're going out for a little action.

Actually a man can get all the action he could ask for from Hasbro. G.I. Joe in chameleon green crouches mechanically and grunts: "Take the Jeep and get some ammo." I actually look for a Jeep to take. Of course, there isn't any there. The Jeeps are accessories, at double the cost of good old Joe. The 1968 series of Pal Joeys of the Jungle introduced counter insurgencies and germ warfare to the vocabulary of the boys' six-to-twelve bracket.

And the Six Million Dollar Man. My nephew Joby once told me that he wanted to be in a plane crash, so that they could put him together again, just like ole Six Mill. And Timmy, the psychotic six-year-old of the neighbors, daily rams his Six Mill Man into the Planet of the Apes Playhouse, until the playhouse looks like grass shacks at Pearl Harbor circa 1941 or until the Bionic Bulldozer loses its one removable eye, and the orb goes rolling along the carpet, and, of course, the dog scoops it up, and Timmy bites the dog's ears in retaliation.

I never told Shirley this, but I've had a lot of trouble envisioning myself changing diapers. I mean, I gag whenever I get near that certain smell. And I didn't think I could coordinate the diapers themselves. I flunked the tourniquet test in Boy Scouts, so I figured I would do just as well on diapers. Well, Mattel's Baby Alive series taught me differently. The saleswoman at Gimbels showed me how you can feed the little tyke some food and watch its instant digestion and excrement. Abracadabra, there's excrement. Then you get to change the diapers. This saleswoman said that surely I must have seen this wonder advertised on TV. No, I didn't think I had. Well, I probably wouldn't have recognized it anyway, said the saleswoman a little maternally, since you couldn't show the buttocks of a doll on TV. I thanked her profusely for what I considered a keepable comment. It's not every day you get a keepable comment at Gimbels. You can see every last iota of tripe in a heart transplant on some of the doctor shows on TV, but you aren't ever going to see any dolly's back-crack. Like I said, keepable. Anyway, I learned that changing diapers wasn't so tough, and if Shirley and I could just teach our baby to digest spontaneously on the spot, there wouldn't be any smell to worry about either.

The saleswoman explained the dolls, but I could see she wasn't really very enthusiastic. In fact she was downright unpleasant and radical, political, critical of the whole plastic practice. They're disgustingly middle class, she said. The boy dolls are all macho creeps. The little ladies are all blond bombshells with blue eyes, and their Aryan measurements, if computed to adult size, would add up to something like 37—21—32. Have you ever known a woman like this? she asked me frontally. I thought of Shirley and wondered for the first time what exactly were her measurements while pregnant. If deflated, what would her measurements be, I was thinking. But the saleswoman had gone on without me. Maybe it was because I was a man, and she didn't think it really mattered to me anyway. How about all the beauty parlors and mobile campers and other capitalist accessories? she was asking rhetorically. And how about that little twit Hugo, the man (doll) of a thousand faces? Wasn't that encouraging a double standard, nay, a thousand standard? And how about the plain sexist discrimination in the fact that one could mail-order the positive boy-toy, the Baby Brother of Skipper, equipped with genitalia, the real thing, but one couldn't mail-order any female dolls with corresponding life-size cavernalia? Outrageous, she said.

When I was a little boy growing up in a stereotypical midwestern small town, I had lots of brothers but no dolls. None of us ever had any dolls until we had a baby sister. The seventh child had been a girl and she had a doll named Elmer. He didn't have any balls, to put it plainly, but he had a great wedge in his lips. My brother Don used to stick my mother's burning Salem cigarettes into Elmer's mouth until they burned scabs on his lips. Jo would watch impotently, screaming at these atrocities but incapable of aiding her Elmer. Now she's twenty-one, still unmarried, and has two obsessions: she wants to have babies and she hates cigarettes.

Shirley asked me if we shouldn't be thinking about a second child. I hadn't really sat down to think about the first one. She said it was a shame with only children, the way they were forced to relate to adults, the way they were deprived of a peer group. Besides, studies have shown— And I forget what the tail end was. I kept thinking of the armies of dolls awaiting a baby in its crib before it's born, thinking of how women share maternity clothes, baby clothes, strollers, snugglies, and bassinettes, thinking of how, when the man is included and the focus is on the newborn, they share stuffed animals and wind-up Willie Wetdreams. How could any child be an only child with all these dolls hanging around like high school dropouts? Surely Shirley was overreacting.

I have a friend named Ted who teaches in an alternative kindergarten. He teaches the kids who flunked *Sesame Street* and *The Electric Company*. He told me that he had a little left-hander in his class that couldn't write for Rudy, that's how he put it. Couldn't move the pencil without qualifying for the adult dosage of tranquilizers. So Ted has this bright idea. He gets the tot's mommy, who wants her tot to be able to jot, of course, to buy the tot the Writing Doll. The doll's hands are flexible and move the pencil very well, as long as the little tot gets behind the doll and holds the hand that holds the pencil with its own human hand. Pretty soon, the tot is writing ten-page letters to the grandparents, all via the dolly. Ted's bright ideas often backfire like this. The mother has sunk twenty dollars into a Writing Doll that would make Bennett Cerf roll over and jump for joy underground, but her little tot will be a missive cripple for life.

Shirley wants something else besides chicken soup for supper. The closer we get to the birth, the more aggressive she becomes in her demands. She soothes me by saying that it's not just for her. If it were for her, she laughs, she would just as soon eat Fritos and Velveeta. But it's for our little one, and I want our little one to grow up to be a healthy big one, don't I? I begin to wonder how demanding the little voice inside her big voice can be. I mean, suppose there are 217 different main courses on the embryo's menu. I'll have to buy one of those microwave ovens. I'll probably get a heart attack from cooking with all that radiation.

"What are you thinking about, dear?"

"I'm going out for a little action."

I ask the saleswoman at Gimbels if there are any alternatives to dolls. What do kids do when they're too old for dolls? Do they then qualify for sex and pot?

"Are you trying to have an affair with me, buster?"

I had never thought of it that way. I realized that someone working in the doll department like that, well, she must get some pretty interesting propositions. Instead of answering, I immediately imagine her without any clothes on, me on top, our bodies glued together with a mechanical precision unknown before the Industrial Revolution, our lips metallic and banging together with the boisterous crunch of burned-out trucks at a demolition derby, our tongues of cinder touching like two Egyptian pyramids tipped on their sides, our elbow joints screaming for more axle grease as they crane, each around the other's plastic neck, thick and hollow as a box of drinking straws . . .

"Say, what are you thinking about, mister?"

"I'm out for a little action."

Obviously my vocabulary is much more limited than that of Nancy Nonsense. The saleswoman's name is Nancy (where did I learn that?), and it takes me twenty minutes to convince her that there was no nonsense intended in my remark. At the end of the twenty minutes Nancy is convinced and somehow disappointed.

"They go to games when they're too old for dolls."

Nancy has a way with words. She gives her radical-political-critical rap on games, beginning with the "super" of them all. Did I know that three and one half million sets of Monopoly were sold annually? No. Living up to their name, I thought. That eighty million sets of Monopoly had been sold since 1935? That was a keepable question, I thought. It suggested that Monopoly's grass roots were in the Depression. I could see it all flash before my eyes. Gangster films for the adults and Monopoly sets for the kids. Instant riches for the hopelessly poor. Why, Nancy said with all the spontaneity of a rehearsed PTA speech, they print up more money than the U.S. Treasury. They teach real estate and private property. They reinforce packratting, the accumulation of material goods, the consumer society. And stratified social classes. Why, when would Baltic Avenue ever be worth anything? And there was welfare, the two hundred dollars every time you passed Go. And there was jail and bankruptcy and even cognitive dissonance, since the Monopoly railroads are worth a lot, while the real railroads are worth less than Baltic Avenue. I was really getting interested in Nancy. I never figured out whether it was because I secretly craved her ball-bearing breasts under all those soft blouses or because she knew so much about games.

Shirley had a game waiting for me when I came home from getting all my Gimbels action. It's called labor. When her water sack broke, I wondered if Mattel would ever manufacture a pregnant Barbie who could break her water sack. As long as TV standards were the way they were, they probably wouldn't. And when our baby came out with a rubber suck, with the same sounds as a skin diver peeling off his/her rubber suit, I knew that I couldn't explain away this flesh and blood with wooden fantasies. Instead of dolls' faces, I could see only forests of blinding green southern pine trees, senselessly chopped down for some Pinocchio whim, a lie that extended further than the smells of synthetic sawdust in the nose. I could smell Shirley's blood and my own underarm sweat from holding her so close for countless hours. I could smell the blue on the baby's face and taste the vernix on the baby's skin. I could feel the wrenching tear in Shirly's perineum when the baby's head came twisting through, molded to whatever shape its mother's doorway presented. I suddenly remembered the names that Shirley and I had decided upon, and they were real names, not Ken or Barbie or Tiffany Taylor or Dizzy Lizzie.

"What are you thinking about, dear?"

"I don't remember."

It was Shirley, and I knew I could live contented with her questions and her chicken soup fevers in this city without trees, because I had already forgotten every doll I'd ever known with one top-of-the-lungs scream from our stringless offspring. And I realized (the final keepable comment) that all the nine months of mannequin madness in imagined undressings of a stainless-steel Nancy Nonsense at Gimbels and this doll delirium that ends with a Pinocchio in pewter in the radical-political-critical modern city of plastic playhouse skyscrapers for a planet of apes without trees was necessary, because I was a man who would never experience the coming of a child through my cavernalia. It was the price I had to pay for the delicious amnesia that was my afterbirth.

"I don't remember."

The Woman at the Well

*J*ESUS met the woman at the well. He is supposed to have said "Woman, woman, you've got five husbands" three times before adding, ". . . and the one you're with, he ain't your own." To me it is the most powerful tale about Jesus ever told, more powerful than bringing Lazarus back to life, more powerful than the Resurrection even. It makes me think of my mother.

It may never have happened, but let us suppose it did. Who can it possibly hurt, this many centuries later? Of course Jesus wasn't speaking English. And I don't know why he insisted that the woman had five husbands three different times, except that three times have always been necessary in Western folklore before one could deliver the punch line. I don't even know what the woman was doing at the well, whether she was there to draw water or using the well as a rendezvous with her hypothetical lover or whether she had delusions of grandeur and wanted to be intimate with Jesus. I don't know anything about the woman at the well, except that she reminds me of my mother.

This is the first time I've ever tried to tell a parable. I feel very awkward with the elliptical turn of phrase and the slow slide into oblique and enigmatic truths. It's a little like learning how to lie again.

My mother had seven children, all with the same husband. I was the third of seven, a fact significant for the numbers themselves, since my parents have been married thirty-seven years. My mother is witty and French-Canadian, so the two have always been synonymous for me. She sometimes speaks directly from the subconscious. Her outrageous comments to complete strangers come pouring out without hesitation, followed by laughter, inevitable low laughter, the thick rasp of bass drums in her lungs. It is not essential that anyone else laugh with her. My father often didn't. I usually did. She still calls me long distance to tell me a joke that would be too dumb to get any response from my father. There is laughter, and then we hang up, so why does she remind me of the woman at the well?

And who is this woman with pressed hair about her temples, standing near the cash register, but not directly in the line to pay? It is in a new restaurant in the shopping center called "The Wishing Well." There isn't any well in the restaurant, but there is a little fountain in the center, and the tables are arranged in circles around the little fountain. You can throw pennies in the fountain. I am here with my infant son, John. John is three months old and has just begun to stare in earnest, to fix peoples' faces with his wide and wondering eyes. We sit at the table nearest the door, so that John won't bother anyone if he cries. I eat my food in a hurry, because John is still breastfeeding. In case he gets hungry, I want to be ready to go. The cash register is across from our table, on the other side of the door. She stands midway between us and the cash register.

I notice her because she stands in the entrance. She is looking neither at us nor at the bill she holds in her left hand. I give in to a fantasy. She may not have enough money to pay her bill, but it is also clear that she has a strong moral character. So she hesitates in the entrance, wanting to pay and wanting to go. She has pressed hair about her temples, obviously combed back with vigor to keep her ears exposed. Yet the rest of her hair is neither gray nor pressed. It is on the verge of breaking into a frizz. This chaos in the hair is the only clue to the woman's desperation. I think it ironic that little John intensely stares at the red plastic flowers on our table, while this middle-aged woman is playing hopscotch with her eyes. She cannot seem to focus. Her eyes are wild, the wild eyes I had associated with children before becoming a father. There is a contradiction in those eyes. They are wild because of their movement, but these eyes seem worn like secondhand clothes. They seem tired of so many years of contact with the light. They are rusty brown, the color of old nails.

Her lipstick is too dark for the pale cheeks. It seems slightly smeared, but perhaps that is due to movement too. Their quiver is almost imperceptible but constant. She looks quickly at little John, and her brown eyes seem to melt, their color spiraling in pools of bright brown glare, the color of fresh dog manure on a summer lawn. She looks back down at the tops of her shoes, and again I am reminded of children, the way they look down when they are being scolded.

My mother has curly hair, blue eyes, and she never wears lipstick. So why do I think of my mother when I look at this woman?

The woman still has not paid her bill. I wonder if I should offer to help her. I wonder how long she has been standing there and whether or not anyone else has noticed her. I look down at John in his carrying seat. I am surprised he is there, he is independent of me, he is mine. Usually when I take my eyes off him, I can still see him. If I take my mind off him, I am surprised to find him there when I come back. How long has he been there? I wonder. I realize that my concentration on the woman has made me lose track of time. I look at my watch. I am curiously aware that this looking at my watch is somehow a signal for the woman with pressed hair about her temples.

She walks up to our table and never once looks at me. Her eyes are on John, her fingers are already gripping the edge of his seat, itching to touch the soft skin beneath the baby clothes. Again I have the distinct feeling of a signal. Her touching the edge of the carrying seat is a signal for me, I sense. For the first time I notice she has breasts. I am surprised that they seem rather round and full for a woman that age. I am surprised too that I have not noticed them before.

"How old?"

She stares with a smile at John, still not looking at me. Of course, she expects me to answer the question, but her eyes are asking John.

"Three months last Sunday."

"What a beautiful, beautiful boy. Yes, I know you're a little boy. You're a picture, little fellow. What's his name?"

"John."

I answer mechanically. I detect a little impatience, maybe even anger in my voice. Am I a little jealous of this stranger addressing my son with the instant lilt of intimacy in her voice? Or jealous that she has gotten his attention away from the plastic flowers? Or angry at him, because now he is returning her smile with his big gummy grin, the grin of no teeth and all warmth?

"After you?"

"Ma'am?"

"Is he named after you?"

"No, ma'am."

It would have cost me nothing to elaborate. But I must have been determined that the private ritual of our naming our son, naming him even so common a name as John, should not be as easy for her to get as the baby's smiles. It was clear that this woman had borne children. She had the look, she even had the smell of a mother to her.

"Would you like to hold him?"

"Oh could I? Could I really?"

My question was loaded. Having deprived her of the reasons why we had named our son John, I somehow felt compelled to compensate by offering her this chance to cradle our baby. I felt awful. I realized that I was using John, who couldn't complain anyway, to assuage my own guilt. I wished she had just looked at him, paid her bill, and left. But she stayed, her eyes enthralled, the way eyes look in front of a candle.

They were smiling at each other, and I sat there

wondering when she would look at me, when she would acknowledge my presence there, as if her looking at me would put her back at her own middle age again. She should have known better, I thought. But she was just as susceptible to his smiles and frowns as we were. She couldn't help feeling that John's smiles meant approval of her or that his sudden frowns meant he was displeased with her. At three months a baby's smiles and frowns are as free as the weather and intended for no one in particular, not even for the mother who gives the life-milk of her breast.

"I like holding them so. After all these years, it's still magic to hold one. You think they're too little to feel anything or give you anything. Then you pick them up and it all comes back to you. It all comes over you, you'll see when he's grown up. It makes me want to cry that mine ever grew up. If you saw them now, you'd never know they were once just as precious and made to hold as this one."

"How many children do you have?"

"Five. All grown. All grown and gone. The only way they'll ever know how I felt is to hold their own someday. Well, thank you."

"You can hold him longer if you like."

"Thank you, but it's enough. It gets too painful after a while."

Suddenly she looked at me, flush in the face, eager to find some understanding in my face. Her eyes had that wet brown glare again. Lovingly brown, like the fur on certain dogs after they've had a bath. I was embarrassed that this first look between us should be so charged with emotion.

"Well, good-bye. You can be very proud. He's a prince."

She walked away, and I pretended to look at John so as not to look at her. I never noticed whether she paid her bill or not. I dropped three brown pennies in the little fountain before I left. I wished her well, nothing very specific, just the wish that she might carry John's image around in her mind for a moment when she might need it.

My mother had seven children of her own. It was awkward for me to feel bypassed by her, more awkward to see her holding John as if he were hers. My wife was tired from the breast-feeding and went to bed every night at eleven during our visit. My mother and I would stay up talking, but I suspect she really stayed up to hold John when he cried. She would swaddle him in his blankets, pull down on the squat little legs, and cradle him over the top of her shoulder while she rocked him, singing low, throaty French songs of sleep. *"Fais dodo,"* she would sing. "Go to sleep, little one." Once, when my mother was in the kitchen fixing supper, I wrapped John in his blankets, cradled him in the same way over my shoulder, rocked him, and sang the same French songs. It didn't work.

My mother and I went through her old photograph albums, looking at pictures of seven children as children. I told her I would take some of them and make duplicates for her and for my brothers and sisters. They were old photographs, but the black-and-white images were still crisp, still in good condition. I sent her these duplicates along with recent pictures of John. She preferred the pictures of the baby, even though the color wasn't true and probably wouldn't last.

During our visit she kept saying that she could really make something of John, if we would only leave him with her for about nine years. At first, it was a joke and everyone laughed. But she kept saying it, even when my father said she shouldn't say such things, and my wife felt a little angry and withdrawn. I only felt embarrassment, which is perhaps an emotion between the other two.

We left on a Sunday morning. That Sunday night my mother called us long distance. She was crying. She said that they had returned from taking us to the airport, and their house had suddenly seemed too big, too empty. She said that she had noticed the crease in the pillow on the couch where John's head had been, and she cried.

So Jesus met the woman at the well. I think it's significant that the woman never has a name. She's just "the woman at the well." Part of her compelling power, I think, comes from her association with the well. It's a fertility symbol. The womb. It's also a symbol of barrenness. It's a death symbol, the suicidal sinking into self.

When Jesus met the woman at the well, I think he was determined to make an example of her. I don't think he was condemning her for being there with someone who wasn't her husband. He certainly forgave worse transgressions in Mary Magdalene. I think it was the five husbands that made him furious. But what does this have to do with my mother, who has been married only once in thirty-seven years?

Shortly after the birth all of my wife's dreams were about her own mother. For some reason it was psychically important for my wife to make this transfer with her mother, to become one with the mother of oneself. It's an awkward turn of phrase, but it's the only way to express this jump in generations. It's the only way to understand why my wife suddenly stopped fighting the influence of her mother. Suddenly her mother became venerable, for all her faults. She became mortal. And so my wife began to treat her mother a little like a daughter. I never understood why my own mother ever permitted my grandmother, even though I was my grandmother's favorite, to come and live with us after my grandfather's death. I blamed my mother, as if she were somehow responsible for my grandmother living twenty more years, draining my mother's energy. The "youth" of my mother's early middle age was spent on my grandmother's indomitable urge to live a life that was no longer worth living. My grandmother was senile and a little insane when she died. She accused my father of stealing her money, while she sobbed like a baby to my mother about the intravenous feeding and the catheter tubes inserted to help her pee. I know now that my mother will be grieving her mother to the grave, and perhaps that's a part of post-partum depression, this grieving for one's loved ones in a past life.

I have repeatedly told my mother that I would put her in a home before I would let her come live with us. These statements are always followed by hollow laughter. I still say these things to my mother, but they are no longer funny, and the words have no force behind them.

When Jesus met the woman at the well, I think it was the five husbands that made him furious. God the Father told Adam and Abraham and Moses and all the other patriarchs to increase and multiply. It was his way of keeping the patriarchy going, by encouraging these wizened old men to get their women perpetually with child. I think it's important that it was Jesus who met the woman at the well, because Jesus was living proof that God the Father and the Holy Spirit had increased and multiplied themselves, even though it was an only-begotten son, conceived under slightly bizarre circumstances.

So what was the woman's crime, after all? Precisely that at the "fertility symbol" of that well Jesus made it plain that she had increased and multiplied husbands, not children. So why does she make me think of my own mother, who had seven children of her own with but one husband?

My mother had seven children, and still it was not enough. It's embarrassing to see her acting like someone who was childless all her life every time she gets near a baby. She has the same loving greed in her eyes, the same hormonal need to mother, even though the time of mothering is long past. Little children are shocked at the sight of a dead bird's body. Their parents are often more shocked by the empty nest. It is a shock that can never be survived. It can only be hidden. Mother-in-law jokes are one such disguise.

When John was five months old, I happened to return with him to The Wishing Well again. He was too big for the carrying seat. I carried him strapped to my back. When I realized where we were, I looked around, expecting to see the woman. Not finding her, I was surprised to see her in the entrance, once we were seated. There was the same untamed concentration in her eyes, the brown color of old nails. There was the same shuffling of the lips, as though they were feet, awkward and gangling like the lips of a teen-age girl. I felt warm all over to see her again, as though she were a long-lost friend. I smiled invitingly at her, but she didn't see my smile. She was staring at John.

She came to our table and looked upon him lovingly, her fingers rubbing the folds of his sleeves.

"How old?"

She still had not looked at me, had neither recognized me nor the baby. I was hurt.

"Five months."

Here I was, being curt again. Why wasn't she looking at me?

"What's his name?"

"John."

"After you?"

"No, not after me. After his mother. His mother's name is Johanna."

"That's very nice."

"Yes, and my grandmother on my father's side, her name was Johanna too."

"You don't say. Well, he's a beautiful, beautiful little boy."

Why was I bothering to explain all this to her now? She clearly wasn't hearing a word I said. She was just looking, her fingers rubbing the folds of his shirt sleeves, like she was fingering a rosary, bead by bead. She just looked and licked him with her eyes.

"He's so very beautiful."

"You should have seen him when he was born."

"Is that so? My, my, he must have been a sight. I don't remember what my children looked like when they were born."

I knew better than to ask, but I felt compelled to follow the rules of this ritual, to respond to her signal.

"How many do you have?"

"Four? Yes, four."

I wanted to scream "five" in her face. How could she lie to me, a complete stranger, an old friend? But maybe she was already a little senile. Maybe she really had forgotten how many. Suddenly I felt very chilled. Maybe she had never had any children.

"Would you like to hold him?"

"Oh, I really shouldn't, but could I? Oh, thank you."

Her brown eyes beamed the grateful, embarrassing lollipop look of a puppy whose chin has just been stroked.

"They grow so fast, these precious little ones."

She was looking at me, eyes to eyes. Blank. Without recognition. I could excuse the fact that she had not remembered John, for he had changed considerably in two months. But I hadn't changed, she hadn't changed, it was the same table with the same red plastic flowers. How could she help but remember?

I threw no pennies in the little fountain after she left. I must have had a troubled look when I paid my bill.

"Was everything all right, sir?"

It was the cashier, a man, perhaps the manager. He was dressed in a suit. He seemed familiar somehow, although there was nothing memorable about him. Then again, he had the small and tidy look of the men who carried the casket at my grandfather's funeral. If it hadn't come to me, I wouldn't have said anything.

"Well, there is something. I don't know if you noticed the woman, a moment ago, at our table?"

"Oh, her."

"You know her?"

"Not exactly. But then everybody knows her in a way. You must not come here very often or you'd know her too."

"I don't understand."

"She's something of a joke. An oddball, you know

what I mean? She's the professional baby-holder. Comes in here every day, hangs around, waits for people with babies to come in. She holds 'em all, that one. Just holds 'em. Nothing harmful in that, I guess, so we don't kick her out or make a fuss. I'm sorry if she offended you."

"No, it's not that. On the contrary. I liked her. I liked her a lot."

When Johanna and I told my mother about the birth, she was amazed and a little frightened by the meticulous details, by the strength of the memory. She confided to us that she had almost no remembrance at all of her seven births. In those days it was common practice for doctors to give scopolamine to women in delivery. The common name for this drug is "twilight sleep." It enabled women of my mother's generation to forget pain. It's not just that they didn't feel pain. They forgot it. Their eyes became extra sensitive to light, so that lights needed dimming. The rails on the delivery table needed to be up, because twilight sleep induced a kind of madness in the women. Under its influence they were capable of doing anything, saying anything. Because their innermost hostilities were no longer inhibited under the influence of the drug, husbands had to wait outside, had to watch through glass, while perfect strangers peeked into these women's most private parts.

What difference is there, after all, between the woman who met Jesus at the well, the woman who keeps waking up each day for the chance to hold other peoples' babies, and my own dear mother alone in her rocking chair, singing French songs to herself long after my father has gone to bed, engulfed as they are in twilight sleep?

Miriam's Delirium

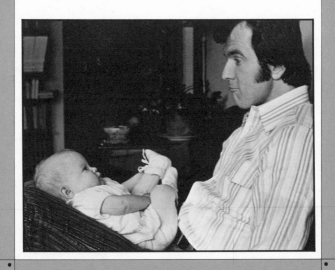

*M*IRIAM found out that she was pregnant on a Tuesday afternoon at 3:30. I remember it well. It was the beginning of the month, the third straight month without blood. We celebrated. We went to Danny's Steak and Tail Shop. I had prime rib. Miriam, undecided after two hours of minute menu-reading, ordered lobster. It was a mistake. We should never have gone.

Pregnant women are more finicky than cats when it comes to food. Especially in the first three months, those months of daydreaming on long-distance telephone calls, months of twenty trips to the bathroom each night, months of empty supper plates and elaborate foods gone stale in the refrigerator. Perhaps it was Miriam's revenge for what has sometimes been called "the woman's curse." Whatever it was, it began innocently enough. A little celebration for the baby who would make us a bona fide nuclear family. That's all. But once Miriam had shelled those little red-orange husks of marine delight at Danny's and tasted the texture of white wondrous flesh, savored in chunks as big as ice cubes in those enormous cheeks of hers, she was hooked. It was lobster, lobster, lobster or croak, monsieur. Nothing else would do.

Such a mono diet must spring from a disease. I had read about pregnant women developing cravings for peanut butter, pizza, pickles, and the like. But this obsession for lobster was not only psychically irrational, it was also economically suicidal. When I mentioned our deepening money problems to Miriam, she became openly scornful, reminding me of golf clubs and midget cars, material objects we (I) had once been able to afford. Why lobster? I asked. Our baby must be telling us something, dear. I went back to the books. I learned that the human fetus did indeed go through the fish stage, sprouting gills before ears, fish eyes before eyelids and brows, maybe even fins before a spinal column. So Junior was a cannibal. But by the beginning of the fourth month, that stage is supposed to have passed. I prayed for a sign that our baby was human. Any sign. Like Miriam wanting tuna fish instead of lobster.

No such luck. The lobster fits continued. At approximately $9.95 per fit. My own eating habits slid down the ladder of nutrition as Miriam's persisted. I went from prime rib to hamburger, from hamburger to homemade sandwiches, to peanut butter, pizza, and pickles. I began to wonder if I weren't the one who was pregnant. Or ulcerous. At first I would feign stomachaches in the restaurants, telling the waiters and waitresses to bring Miriam's lobster while I deliberated. My mouth watered for food, but not for her endless graveyard of red shells. I began to wonder if her bowel movements (lobster aids elimination) weren't higher in protein than most people's weekly diet. I began to wonder if her urine weren't turning more and more yellow from all the lemon butter.

—Why lobster, Miriam? I think it was about halfway through the fourth month that I asked. I could hear the little bugger squishing in her cavernous cheeks as she answered. Butter was dripping down her chin. —I'm going through a stage, she answered. Something about all mothers reliving the lives of their mothers, their own births. That's what motherhood meant, then. Where was all this in the books? —Mother never had enough to eat, she suggested mournfully between bites, her napkin going up and down from her lap to her mouth like a ship trying to surrender. —That's why I've always been so thin. —You can understand that, dear. And if I couldn't understand, did that mean I was the typical insensitive husband, yearning for Tahiti instead of for Junior? I became silent, pondering extra jobs to pay for these gargantuan meals. The telltale cadavers of red shell were testimony to a marine holocaust. She was depleting the ocean, that's all I could think about. Naturally I thought ecologically instead of economically. What the Russians and Japanese were doing to the whale, my wife was doing to the lobster. Soon Cannery Row would be a ghost town.

For all that ingested sea life, Miriam did not change her daily routine. In the morning she would haphazardly make the bed, sink into a swoon until about ten o'clock, call me at work in a panic about what she should eat for lunch. When she couldn't get me, she'd call her mother in Kenosha long distance. The phone bills mounted even more astronomically than the food bills. Miriam justified this expense by saying that it was absolutely essential that she know every detail surrounding her own birth, so that her delivery would be "made in heaven" (her phrase, not mine). So I paid for any hesitations in my mother-in-law's memory.

Supper time was the moment of terror. The moment when the sun went down, when vampires went off in search of blood, Miriam got the itch for thermidor. She just couldn't stomach cooking at home. She tried and botched it. When she could manage a full meal, I raved and raved about how delicious it was. She watched me for a minute or so, then went off to throw up. The sound of her raw throat gasping for air above the toilet bowl always took away my appetite. So I would try the cooking. —What would you like tonight, my sweet? Baked chicken, Chinese cabbage, beef stew, fresh garden salads: I tried them all. When I'd gotten through a half-hour recitation of possible dinners and had gotten a faint "maybe" or "yes" from Miriam, I worked myself silly over fixing the meal, only to find that Miriam had changed her mind when the plate was inched in front of her. She would cry, and when the words were intelligible, they were to the effect that I didn't love her. Then she'd go off to bed, uprooting all the covers, burying herself in the fetal position. When I would come to bed, there would be bare sheets and no pillows waiting for me.

Money is such a sad issue to fight about, and such a sorry way to keep from fighting. But I became a coward.

Our nine ninety-five truce, I came to call it. What else was there to do? Miriam was a diseased woman. Miriam's delirium, I called it. Not to her face, of course.

Have you ever stopped to figure out how much a marriage based on lobster could cost at $9.95 per day for a week? A month? Nine interminable lobster-littered months? I began to wonder (with the aid of a pocket calculator I bought for the purpose of wondering with some accuracy) whether or not alimony and child support wouldn't be cheaper in the long run than night after night of devouring the protein king of the sea.

—Miriam, aren't you worried about the cholesterol level in our unborn baby? Tears and sobbing, the wiping of eyes, inflamed by the splotches of lemon butter on the napkin. I was driving her mad. She always beat me to it, reversing whatever I happened to be thinking at the moment. I would look at her as though she were the Queen of Mars, some body-snitching goddess grown bulbous in the belly who had taken over my poor unassuming Miriam, whose only trauma in life prior to the pregnancy had been the realization that she was not the prototypical Jewish princess, because her starving mother had not fed her enough gefilte fish when she was growing up. I would stare at this Queen of Mars over candlelight (Miriam had tired of Danny's, so we'd gone "uptown" to La Poisson Soluble, where the lobster rang up at $14.95), and she would look up and stare back, accusing me of bags under my eyes, craters, the man-in-the-moon look. —What's gotten into you? she'd beat me to asking. Hell, I didn't need to ask. I already knew the only thing that had gotten into Miriam for the past six months.

I began to pout openly, to look for fights to pick with Miriam, to look for excuses to break the unused supper plates, to spill the unemptied garbage pails.

—Why lobster, my little myrmidon? —It's cheaper than a shrink, you nasty bastard, she'd snort. And the sound would echo through the heap of hollowed shells.

. . . I began to read the newspaper when the lobster came. One day I read about some college kids at Yale who'd broken the world record for swallowing goldfish. It's a pathetic world, I thought. End of newspaper. I preferred watching Miriam.

I had not deserved a raise. In fact my work had been steadily slipping for about three months. But my boss, a father of seven, knew it was my first time, assumed I wanted to buy hobbyhorses and baseball bats, and he gave me the raise. For every raise there's a drop. That's the dictum around our office. The boss berated Laskey. —More production, Laskey, more output, you drone. I felt like Judas. Laskey had been covering for me for months, doing his share of the sales and then some for me. For every raise there's an elbow. Laskey jerked his in my sides on the elevator ride down to lunch. — What's it for, you creep, he winked with those sotted eyes of his. I felt better. Laskey's raises always went flushabye down the john at Barney's Bar and Grill. —For lemon butter, I answered. —Jesus, went a lackluster Laskey, your guts must be brown from all that boss-wipe.

Why lobster, Miriam? The endless refrain to my bankrupt litany. The only difference when I prayed was the substitution of "God" for "Miriam" on the end.

In the beginning of the seventh month I began to have an acne problem. I had never had a problem with pimples, not even as an unloved, overly-masturbating teenager. At the age of thirty-three one doesn't expect a crop of red pus-poppers. It's undignified. Laskey spread this talk of venereal disease on the job. He's got the pox, Laskey hissed in every corner. When the secretaries went *dot-dot-dot* on the IBMs in the morning, it sounded like "he's got the pox" to me. Miriam would call for her daily dilemma about lunch, and I could still hear typewriters, gossiping like snakes in those pregnant midmorning silences. —Go to hell, I said to Miriam in the same controlled business-pitch with which I'd tell the secretaries to "take a memo." When I got home, I'd find Miriam in the bathtub and the carcasses of some fifteen deviled eggs in the kitchen. Miriam had eaten the yellows, left the whites.

I forgot to mention one effect that this lobster-mania had had on our daily lives. Our water bill had gone up. Miriam took three and sometimes five baths a day, the three extremities of her body bobbing on top of the water like buoys in a tidal creek: her head, her belly, and her toes. Junior looked like a bowling ball with one filled-in hole for the thumb. I could envision Miriam rolling down the lane with Junior inside, the pins like stacked Coke bottles at the other end of the alley, waiting to be cracked and shattered.

KERRAACK (Strike) *KEEESSSHHH* (glass) *SSSSSSHHHHHH* (like the tinkling of a mobile).

—Clummox! This was Miriam with her knife in one hand and the fork in the other. I had just elbowed her lobster Kiev and her carafe of burgundy out of the waiter's arms and onto the floor. We would have to wait for another. Junior was probably barking with expectancy inside. Cold turkey, Junior.

In the beginning of the eighth month Miriam began her bouts with anemia. I felt sorry for her, the kind of sorry you feel for Charlie Chaplin every time he trips on his own baggy pants. You still laugh. Yawning from those cheeks so cavernous they could propel a sailboat on a still day, Miriam looked like a sleepwalker. A zombie. A pumpkin face. Grocery shopping, she looked so non-chalant and slow-moving compared with all the other housewives in curlers who did their Indy 500 with shop-carts. Miriam spilled the whole kit-'n'-caboodle of red running apples when she picked one from the bottom. They seemed to be falling from the mirror behind and above too. I felt sorry for her standing there looking at the floor full of Jonathans, Winesaps, and Red Romes. She looked like she had just been caught trying to shoplift a watermelon under her "preggy" pants with the stretch flap in front like a bib on a nun. Poor Miriam, I thought, as I grabbed three packets of frozen lobsters.

—Not enough iron, the doctor had said. —More iron, Miriam, I chimed like a cuckoo clock. More iron, Miriam, had almost become as prevalent as Why lobster, Miriam. Miriam's mother threatened to come every day. It was a dilemma for me. It would save on phone calls. It would free me from cooking, cleaning, running bathwater, and shucking lobster shells. But it would drive me mad from the meddling. It was then I realized why I disliked Laskey so much. He reminded me of my mother-in-law. Both were the kind of people who lean over battered bodies in the middle of the street and say: "You shouldn't jaywalk."

It was the time of strategic coaching. The man's role in any pregnancy is at best a little mythical. He can either spend the whole nine months building birdhouses in the backyard or he can coach with a "Yes you can, Miriam" rejoinder at the appropriate times, like a cheerleader at a high school football game whose team is losing forty to zero. —Yes you can, yes you can . . . hey hey what do you say, get that ball and fight . . .

—What do you mean, "Get that ball and fight?" — I'm just trying to take a shit, you neon blink. I was sitting on the edge of the tub, running Miriam's water, encouraging her to do battle with her constipation.

The constipation was a real issue during the last months. We were near bankruptcy from the lobster orgies, I was trying to figure out how to get Junior delivered under a false name and sneak Miriam out of the hospital with the watermelon under her drawers, trying to imagine Miriam selling Tupperware, and Junior with a paper route to help pay for his entry into this pathetic world, and Miriam sits there on the stool like a striking cow. No milk, madame, no turds today. Stuck with all that trapped gas inside. And Junior kicking like some Thai boxer at her walls.

The breathing exercises, for which I was to do the

coaching (one two three, one two three, hey hey what do you say), were a problem for Miriam, because of all the bloating.

—You know what it's like? she was asking me, her feet propped up on the wastebasket in front of the toilet seat, looking like a mix-up in the freefall exercises between parachutes and bombs. —You want to know what it's like, goddamn it, or don't you? Her cheeks were ruddy red and inflamed from so much grunting. —It's like a ketchup bottle when you open it. —You turn it upside down, you bang the damn bottle with both fists trying to get a crummy drop and then when you're just about ready to give up it whooshes like a fountain. —I can't go because of this kid. —I wish I could just whoosh him through the tubes, you know? —I feel like a Goodyear blimp. —Don't you dare laugh. —I wish you could stick a needle in me and let the air out. —I never wished for diarrhea so bad in all my life.

It was the most communication we'd had in seven months. Strained and surly, nearly broke and reeling from the upcoming debts, we had almost divorced in the seventh month. Like the parting of the Red Sea, I'd felt for seven months like I was a herd of Egyptians chasing after Miriam and her tribe, standing flatfooted on a dry seabed and wondering when's it gonna pour, my Lord, when's it gonna pour.

I fell in love with Miriam, sitting there stuck on the stool in the beginning of the eighth month. She had been dependent on me throughout the pregnancy, but this was a different dependency than the usual woman-on-man in the wedded state. She wasn't asking me to be the telephone pole of silent strength telling her to hush, little baby. She wasn't asking me to fetch her pickles in the middle of the night. She wasn't asking me to coach her one-two-three in those mindless mornings of dry labor. She wasn't even asking me to be a man, a father, a stone of Sunday morning sermons. She was telling me what it was like. Woman to woman. Pal to pal. I realized that she was talking to me as she probably would talk to her mother. Like she probably would talk to a midwife. We could again withdraw into that cocoon that only lovers and expectant mothers can know, the withdrawal of silky silent spider's threads, fragile yet firm enough that diamonds can't cut, the cocoon that makes an outsider say— I don't know much about them, but they're thick as thieves, you can see it in their eyes. The cocoon of dried blood around a wound. Like lobsters scurrying on the deaf and dumb ocean floor.

The ninth month passed over us like a vacuum cleaner. We came to terms without incident.

Lie Still

*J*ENNY lies. There's no room for speculation on that point. She's six, overly developed sexually, cute and curt like the frayed whiskers on a female Siamese cat. Even pouting in the hushed secrecy of her bedroom with the Ferris wheels, candy canes, and clowns with cheeks the rainbow colors of Neapolitan ice cream, she's more flirtatious than Dietrich or Garbo under floodlights of fantasy. But Jenny lies. The fact bears repeating, the reminder an insurance against this siren of the fib. How long has she been lying? Since two? Since the end of silence at the nipple? I wonder if there's some connection between the curly hair like cones the way the leaves funnel when they fall and the teasing circular words that soothe because they skirt around, because they smooth over, mentholated white dollops of cream on the red rash of sunburn. I must be more direct.

"Jenny, that's just not true."

"Is so. Is so."

In the very vehemence of rebuttal, the truth. At six. If she were an adult, I wouldn't belabor the point. She's a liar and I won't talk to her ever again. With a six-year-old there's the nagging of the preacher, the little lessons for the road of life, speeches I give for the hearing of them myself, words she doesn't hear, except as jibberish, Alice in the mirror seeing only grown-ups.

I haven't told her mother this. When her mother and my wife go out together, I actually look forward to baby-sitting Jenny, to the chance for confrontation.

"I love you. You can be my husband when I grow up."

"Thank you, Jenny."

Jenny knows how to kill a confrontation before it starts. I'm pleased, I glow, she giggles at my blushing.

Inside I wonder if "I love you" means "I hate you" or "I use you" or something else more menacing. I envision as I glow the primitive wedding ritual of an African tribe, uncivilized, cannibalistic. The taboo of transgression with someone six. Jenny in her white communion dress with the ruffles more curly than her hair. Me as a spear with ribbons and feathers around the wood, my head wobbling like a light bulb loose in its socket at the very top. Thank you, Jenny, but no thanks.

Sometimes I think she deliberately contradicts herself in successive sentences to see if I'm paying attention. Sometimes I think she does it for herself, a kind of private game, playing with all the possibilities out loud.

"I'm forty-eight years old."

"Jenny, you're not. You're six."

"No I'm not. Not. Not. You know why?"

"Why?"

"Cuz my name's not Jenny." (She giggles.)

"That doesn't make sense. Some reason why." (She begins to pick her nose as I say this.) "And stop picking your nose. Little girls don't do that."

"Do little boys?"

"Well no, that's not what I meant. Big people shouldn't do it either."

"When they're forty-eight they can."

"Why?"

"Cuz Jimmy Devlin says his daddy does and he's fifty. Jimmy told him not to, and his daddy said he had to cuz if he didn't he'd get 'our bite us.'"

"What's that?"

"You know, tummyaches in the fingers."

"You mean arthritis?"

"Yes. That's what I said."

You're never right with a child. The first and last lines of any conversation with a six-year-old always go to the six-year-old. If you're forty-eight, you'd best shut up. I have this theory that the terrible twos are nothing compared to the severe sixes. That firmness of conviction before the age of reason. You'd need to be a carpenter to pull out the nails. Or a senile baby-sitting shutter-up.

There are two kinds of liars. Seven is the cutoff point. Before the magic 7 (itself, a bending of the truth), it's playful and encouraged. After that it's perjury, bearing false witness, as under oath. I will not tolerate this double standard. I assume that Jenny knows the difference. She's too clever not to. I won't encourage her. A monster looms inside this midget queen. I tuck her in to sleep.

Ten minutes later in the dark of her room.

"What?"

"Know what I did when you kissed me and left the room?"

"No. What?"

"I picked my nose . . . [pause for invisible giggling] and wiped it on the spot where you kissed me . . . [more giggling] now it's all gone."

"That's nice, Jenny. Now go to sleep. Your mother will be mad if she comes home and finds out you're still awake and I didn't get you to sleep."

"What will you give me if I go to sleep?"

I could feel the flirtation on her face, even though I couldn't see it. Her eyes had to be darting at the chance to barter with a grown-up.

"Another kiss?"

"No, I want a baby."

"Well, let's turn on the light and find your doll."

"No. I mean a real baby."

"You'll have plenty of chances for that when you grow up."

"When I'm forty-eight?"

"No, probably sooner than that."

"When I'm fourteen?"

"No. That's a little too soon."

"Jimmy Devlin says he can give me a real baby right now if I let him ride my bike. Is that a lie?"

When I was growing up, there were two taboos in

our family of seven. You never bit anyone and you never called anyone a liar. My mother would swoop down with the same punishment for either offense. She'd crunch her teeth in our skin until we had a welt to show all the other kids in the neighborhood. The only difference was in position. If you were a biter, she'd bite you back in exactly the same spot you had bitten the brother or sister. If you had said "liar," she'd bite you wherever she could. My younger brother, Don, had a theory about younger brothers being better off than older brothers when it came to moms. He tested that theory repeatedly in our youth. He would suck his arm until the flush began to appear. Then he'd bite down once, quickly, jabbingly, the way a snake springs. The proof at hand, he'd scream to Mother that I had bitten him. Before I could open my mouth, she would have branded me with her gnawing of teeth. None of this "It hurts me more than it does you" stuff. To the skin. And chomp like corn on the cob. I would immediately go numb at the spot. My pride hurting more than my skin, I'd blurt out that Don was a liar. Whammo. Second bite. You can't win with mothers. The first and last bite always go to them.

"Now what, Jenny?"

"I am so forty-eight. I am so."

"Okay, you're forty-eight. Now go to sleep, okay?"

"See? You were lying. I was forty-eight all the time. Even you say so too."

When I remind my mother about those times when Don played me for a double sucker and proved his theories of younger-better at the expense of my mother, she denies it. She laughs nervously and says I'm making it all up. That's her way of saying I'm under the big 7, I guess, because she's really calling me a liar. I think her memory is failing her. She's fifty-two and going through change of life. I suppose that's why.

"Jenny, I may have to spank you if you don't stop calling me in here. There's a time to play and a time to sleep. Now is time to sleep."

"Are you going to sleep with me?"

"No. But I'll be in the next room. You won't be alone."

Or maybe like Jenny I remembered more bites than there really were, more lies than there really were. When I talk to Don now, it seems clear he's revised his theories. Now it's "You got all the good clothes and I got the hand-me-downs, and the folks made the mistakes with you and then clamped down on me." For some reason I don't even know how old Don is.

"Jimmy Devlin says his daddy had a second thought."

"What's that supposed to mean?"

"He asked his daddy how come he got to be his daddy and his daddy said he was a second thought."

"He did not say that, Jenny. He couldn't have."

"Did so. Jimmy said he did."

"Well, Jimmy may be making it up."

"Boys don't make up stories. Jimmy says so. Only girls."

My earliest childhood memory is of when I was four. I had been given a three-wheeler, red and white, with ribbons hanging from the handlebars. My mother told me not to leave our block with it and not to go into the street. I agreed. One day I was riding on the other side of our block from our house. Across the street a little girl wearing taps on her shoes hollers to me that she likes my bike. She has freckles and a big hole where her front teeth should be. I think she's ugly. But I'm excited just the same. You can't touch it, I holler back. Who needs yer old bike anyway, she blasts back. You're a mean boy. I am not. Are so. Am not. Are so. Not. So. Please let me ride your bike. You can touch it but you can't ride it. She crosses the street. Free. Without looking. She's used to it. Suddenly I hate her, because she can cross the street. I changed my mind, you can't even touch it. She's so close to be denied. Liar. You said I could. I changed my mind. Besides, you're ugly. She cries and runs home. My mother met a new neighbor that night. She was always meeting new neighbors.

My wife and I just met a new neighbor. She's a midwife. Now we're thinking of having a baby.

"My mommy says I can have lots of babies when I grow up. And you can be my brother if you want to."

"I'd like that, Jenny. Now sleep."

"My mommy had lots of babies but they died."

"That's a lie."

"She told me so. She had big tummies lots of times. Daddy says they all went to heaven. My daddy's right. He's a boy."

If they're right, which I doubt, boys have a tougher time of it than girls. I wasn't supposed to cry when my mother bit me and Don was laughing behind her back. Sometimes he laughed harder when he saw me crying. Despite what everyone says, maybe it's better to be an only child.

"This is the last time I'm coming in here. The next time you call, I'm going to stay in the other room, because it's time for you to go to sleep."

"Know what?"

"What?"

"My dolly weed on the bed."

Lights on. The changing of sheets and bliss on Jenny's face. No doubt she stuck her finger in her nose and wiped the exact spot where the no-hole doll was supposed to have sprinkled from.

"My mommy says girls have one more hole than boys. We're lucky. We can go potty and have babies too. Boys can only go potty."

We went into the bathroom, pulled down Jenny's pajamas, and washed her legs and genitals. So small, so soft, so perfect to touch. Limpid after rains like April afternoons, that soft. Her little vagina looked like two milk-coated spoons side by side. Someday there would be hair and many men to cry.

"Do you think I'm pretty?"

I think you're a siren. I think that once upon a time we used to be cannibals. We must have been. Why else is there such a thrill to squeeze a baby's toes, to run one's nose up and down a baby's buttocks crack, to nibble gently on the little genitals, to sniff a baby's hair freshly oiled from a bath? Why else do we suck our thumbs, bite our fingernails, chug milk at the breast, gobble food, play with our penises? When we cut our fingers on a piece of glass, we go down on the wound with our mouths and suck the blood. The height of carnal love must be gluttony, the biting, chewing, swallowing of a soul.

"I love you. And you can be one of my babies too. When I grow up."

"Thank you, Jenny."

"Know why I know I'm forty-eight?"

"No. Why?"

"Cuz a long time ago I had many babies. Did too. This many." Crucifixion pose of the arms. "And they had lots of names too. They called me mommy and my name wasn't Jenny. I remember it. And one day they were bad little boys and girls and I ate them all up."

"Jenny, that's the biggest lie I have ever heard."

"My name is not Jenny."

"What is it, then?"

"It's . . ."

"Well?"

"It's . . . [giggling] . . . it's Jimmy."

You've got too many holes to be a Jimmy, I thought. I am aware that baby-sitters should not have fantasies about the children in their care, fantasies in which they envision the children grown up, equals in every way. For love and hate. For sex and death. For forgetting.

"It was long ago."

"How long?"

"Maybe forty years?"

"Jenny, that's not possible. You're only six."

"I know. But I was lots older before I was a baby."

She giggles and sticks out her tongue. I want to

pull her hair. Pull down her pants. Bite her tongue. I bite my own. I can't even tell her she's ugly. She's not and boys don't make up stories.

"When's mommy coming home?"

"Soon I hope."

"Can I stay up to see her?"

"No."

"Can I have some ice cream?"

"No."

"Can I break my dolly's glasses?"

"Your dolly doesn't wear glasses."

"He does so. You can't see 'em, cuz you're not wearing glasses."

"Go to sleep."

"Can I have a glass of water?"

"No. Your dolly might wet the bed again."

"Is my mommy prettier than Nina?"

Nina is my wife.

"They're both pretty. Very pretty, both of them. Now sleepy-poo."

"How come Nina doesn't have any babies?"

Kids come right out and ask the questions without corners. No frosting. No fudge. Straight to the skin. The questions we take years to come around to.

"She's not ready yet."

"Is she fourteen?"

"No, she's twenty-nine."

"That's almost forty-eight, isn't it?"

My mother used to say it didn't matter if you had the money or not and it didn't matter if it was a boy or girl. People should make other people. My mother went to thirteen doctors before she found out she had an acid deposit that was killing off my father's sperm. That was four years into their (I presume) very concerned marriage. They removed the deposit and out came my brother. It became addictive, I guess. Withdraw the deposit (it came back after every birth) and out poofs another brother. Withdraw again and out I came. You think you're so smart, she used to say. If I'd waited like you're waiting, where would you be? Her logic was impeccable. I wouldn't be arguing with you, I'd answer. My answers were never as good as her questions.

"My daddy's dead."

"He is not. Jenny, I'm going to tell him what you said when he gets home. You know very well he's working."

She had told me in a gush of whispering. Sharing her secrets with me. She bit her lip and showed shower forecasts in her baby blues at the vehemence of my answer. I regretted having said it as soon as it was said. To children lying isn't the great sin. Tattling is. Telling on each other. She was used to my accusations but not to my threats of telling. I had betrayed her. She hung her arms in the crucifixion pose.

"When my daddy comes home from work, he always says he's dead. That's why he can't play with me."

The nails must have come undone, because she said this with a shrug of her shoulders. They must have come undone, because I could feel them in me.

"Oh, Jenny, I'm sorry. You weren't lying. I was wrong and you were telling the truth. Come and sit on my lap and I'll sing you a song."

She was still fighting the tears.

"No. I want to go to sleep now."

"Do you want a glass of water first?"

"No."

"Then how about a kiss?"

"No."

"A touch?"

I was losing and I couldn't make myself shut up.

"No."

"Will you say a prayer for me before you go to sleep?"

"No."

"Please?"

Many men would beg to their raw skin, on their

knees like no other genuflection, for a simple "yes" from this child-woman. Many would beg before she would turn forty-eight. And their begging would be the only prayer they would have. Jenny would teach them what it really means to pray, to beg for a touch if not a ride, a look if not a touch. I was sure of it.

No answer. She closed her eyes on me in the dark of her bedroom. I couldn't see them close, but I knew she had closed them. There was no more heat between us. Just a brush of wind. This must be what it's like to sit upon a hospital bed and watch a loved one die. The same cold, same numbness, same frostbite. The same sense of tightening like a rock in the stomach, perhaps in reaction to the other one letting go in the eyes. And that feeling of being ridiculous when suddenly caught talking to myself.

"Lie still now. And don't let any of your sheep stumble."

I never knew what she meant by that. I don't remember ever dreaming about any sheep. All I remember is her telling me, many years later, that I had let this little girl ride my bike and that she had fallen and gone home crying to her mother. So I was punished, not for crossing the street after all, but for having made someone cry.

The Name Game

*T*HIS story is true. Only the names have been changed, to convince the innocent that they may be guilty.

It was the eighth month of our full moonless pregnancy. I who had never gone to bed before midnight now went to bed with Renee at nine or ten. As usual the bed was unmade, the pillows sagged in the middle, the sheets and blankets clung together in knots. And in the dark, not looking at each other, we listened to trains go by outside our window and stared up at the high ceiling for the occasional lights that came and went, distant as prairie fires in late September.

Renee and I had stopped making love around the sixth month. At first it had been my fault. Once, when she had sat on top, I had seen her lower belly move in waves each time that I thrust my entire confused body upward and inward. It was ridiculous, but I believed that I was causing brain damage to the unborn child. Renee said that it was more Freudian than that, that I was seeing her as a mother for the first time, and that I had equated her with my own mother. Perhaps she was right. All I knew was that, for the first time in our five years together, I no longer required her, coveted her, no longer stirred when her body moved, squat and misshapen from the bed to the bathroom some twenty times each night. Normally my snoring didn't bother her. But with these repeated trips to relieve her bladder, she found it more and more difficult to get back to sleep, because of my snoring. So I had moved to the guest room at the end of the sixth month. We now needed two separate bedrooms when we visited my parents. "They sleep in separate bedrooms," my father and mother would whisper to each other, as if they were sharing some soap-opera gossip. From abstinence to absence, we had gotten used to everything, even this pattern of staring at the ceiling, Renee under the covers, me on top of them and still fully clothed, talking instead of touching, waiting for Renee to fall asleep before I went shoeless and alone in the long hallway to the empty unmade bed in the guest room.

We knew these patterns as well as we knew each other's bodies, because fresh habits are as strong as deep memories. We knew, too, that these patterns would continue well after the birth. It would be breast-feeding instead of her bladder that would get Renee up in the night, and my snoring would still be intolerable. It would be physical fatigue and a psychic fear of someone staring at us that would prevent our resumption of sexual intercourse. It would be strangers in the night, one wet nurse waking the other, exchanging two or three hurried words of love and soft complaint, that would make us lose track of how many times the train had passed. We learned to live with these new patterns all in a body, as if they were the new baby, even before and long after its coming.

In the eighth month a new topic surfaced, and we were glad for the break in monotony. Renee suggested that we think of names. We had never before talked about the sex of the child, let alone what name to give. So this was cement. There was no longer any thought of an abortion, a miscarriage, a fever that would run its course and then disappear. A thing does not exist until it has a name. Even stillborns are given a name, so that the parents can embrace a "person" in their grief and their memory. Somewhere between the 9:15 and 9:30 trains, this need to christen had descended upon us, as sudden and as thick as a first snowfall.

I had successfully stripped myself of my ego involvement during the first eight months of the pregnancy. Who was I, after all, to think that I had any control over whether the baby would have ten toes or eleven, blue eyes or brown, acne or measles? Juices stored in me had fertilized an egg stored in Renee. Internal collusion without our foreknowledge. It was as though we belonged to an enormous corporation, in which two stock-holders had suddenly declared dividends for themselves. Such things happen. I am not inventing anything. I had successfully resolved that I would be happy and detached at the moment of birth, letting this miracle from on high splash out as freely as an ocean wave explodes upon a coral reef. Likewise I would take no blame nor place any blame on Renee if the child did emerge with twelve toes or four eyes or whatever other whimsical recipe the gods might concoct out of boredom.

This was before the name game. Whatever else a prospective father or mother has no control over in child-bearing, they do control the name by which this pulp of protoplasm takes shape, grows, defends itself against the world. There can be no more burdensome decision in the entire nine months of a pregnancy than this label affixed to an invisible embryo. Renee was eager to begin this ritual without rules.

I was more skeptical. Naming had always been a disaster in my family. There had been twenty children in my grandmother's family: nineteen girls and one boy. With that many girls some had to have boy's names: Al-freda, Donalda, Roberta. Once their parents had given them these names, their peer group changed them to Fred, Donnie, and Bert. The one boy was named Anthony, which became Peno in that inevitable process by which the name gets smaller as the body gets bigger. Peno had been a lovable, slightly effeminate drunkard and gambler, who married late (his forties) and died early (his fifties). My grandmother had named one of her sons Dranoel, which was Leonard (her last name) spelled backward. Dranoel Leonard. At eighteen he ran away to California, changed his name to Ben, and became an alcoholic. My Aunt Blanche (nicknamed Baba, for "black sheep," since she was indeed the black sheep, and not "blanche" or "white"), named her son Darryl Alphonsus, since his birth day coincided with St. Alphonsus day. He changed his name to Duke as soon as he became of age. My mother, named Dolores ("sorrow"), who has the best sense of humor of any woman I have ever known, named her second daughter Joanne Dolores. In a letter we received during the eighth month, Jo suggested names (first and second, inclusive) that would be acceptable to her for our child. In a P.S., she stated that under no circumstances should we name a daughter Dolores. The psychic weight of a name is infinitely heavier than the physical body weight. Some women, I suspect, get married and change their family names, when what they would really like to change are their first names. Men who as boys joined gangs, played sports, or otherwise sought out other boys invariably changed their names: Wee Willie, Joltin' Joe, Big Al. We spend our lives slaying our parents for the names they dressed us with: pants they put on us with a stuck zipper. I was more skeptical.

Renee and I quickly came up with a few rules. We would not name our child after any relatives, living or dead, or after any friends, living or dead. Not even the middle name would duplicate the living or dead. We would not ask the opinion of any relatives or friends, living or dead. Nor would we pray for a name and expect it to come out when the baby's head did.

We were limited. I had nothing against common names, good old American names, like Tom or Mike or Joe. Renee objected to any name that would be duplicated several thousand times over by every other parent giving birth around the time we did. It had to be an uncommon name, short enough that it couldn't be shortened to a diminutive, strong enough that it wouldn't be changed to a nickname, and free of any cultural associations, so that the child would not, later in life, have to undergo psychoanalysis over the need to live up to a certain name. Kirk was church, no churches. Peter was rock, no rocks. Rose was a flower, no flowers. Guy was a wire, John was a toilet, Harry was hirsute. We had to be careful.

We decided to make separate lists. Those names appearing on both our lists would be kept for further discussion and a later ballot. There would be no discussion about a name appearing on only one of our lists. It seemed simple enough.

Renee chatted while she drew lots, as it were. "I like Margaret," she said, "I've always liked Margaret. But I hate Margo, Margie, Maggie, Mugs." "I've always liked Marshall," I said. "No sheriffs," she said. And we wrote on.

For a boy Renee picked the following: Adam, Adrian, Alan, Austin, Brian, Bruce, Christopher, Daniel, Duncan, Evan, Gary, Glen, Hugh, Ian, Jeffrey, Jesse, Keith, Luke, Lyle, Mark, Nathaniel, Neal, Noel, Patrick, Paul, Russell, Samuel, Scott, Seth, Todd, Vincent, Zachary.

I picked Adrian, Anthony, Alan, Brian, David, Eric, Evan, Geoffrey, Hans, Ian, James, Jeffrey, Jonathan, Kevin, Lars, Mark, Matthew, Paul, Scott, Seth, Stephen, William.

That left Adrian, Alan, Brian, Evan, Ian, Jeffrey, Mark, Paul, Scott, and Seth. We both felt like mass murderers when we compared lists.

We laughed at the rejections. For my part, I mused: Adam, how could you, Renee? Too much like original sin, the garden, snakes. Austin? You mean Texas? Bruce? Loose Bruce got the goose and lost his juice. Foppy name. Christopher? Nobody would bother. Chris. Rhymes with prissy, sissy, Chrissie. Duncan Hines. We're making a baby, not a cake mix. Gary, Indiana. Glen? Hugh? They both sound hollow inside. Jesse? Everyone will think of Jesse James. Luke? Sounds too much like a cowboy or an apostle. Lyle, lyle, crocodile. Nathaniel, too much like Hawthorne, too easily Nat, or Natty Bumpo. Noel, that's either Coward or Christmas.

Renee had her fun at my expense as well. Anthony, no. Not another Peno. I've known too many Davids who were weak men. Eric is nice, but I don't like Ricky. Hans? God, where are the wooden shoes? Jonathan's okay, but people will just call him John or Johnnie. Lars? Never. I like Matt, but not Matthew.

For a girl Renee came up with: Adrienne, Andrea, Belinda, Cleo, Eva, Gwen, Jill, Joyce, Muriel, Nathalie, Olivia, Phoebe, Sybil, Anneke, Emily, Jennifer, Amy, Zoe. I had: Adrienne, Amy, Anneke, Anita, Beth, Cleo, Elizabeth, Emily, Eva, Ingrid, Jennifer, Jessica, Joyce, Kirsten, Miriam, Monica, Nola, Polly, Tina, Zoe.

You picked Muriel? Cigars, honey, that's what people will think. Well, you picked Polly. Wanna cracker? Gwen? Kirsten? It was surprising that we both had picked Joyce. Joyce had been the name of my fiancée once, three years before I met Renee. We were left with Adrienne, Cleo, Eva, Joyce, Anneke, Emily, Jennifer, Amy, Zoe. Why were there so many good choices among the girls's names?

We slept on these names for weeks. We chewed them for supper instead of food. We brushed our teeth with them to see if we could still say them in spite of the brush. We signed these names on the back of the phone bill and gas bill. I came home from work one day, and Renee asked me: "Do you think people would dare to shorten Adrienne to Ad? I couldn't bear it, I just couldn't bear it." I woke Renee one morning to ask her: "Don't you think Seth sounds a little too old English?" If anyone had bugged our phones during that time, he would have gotten only non sequiturs out of us. "Evan is either too much like 'even' or like 'oven.' " "Paul, it's so flat-sounding. You think of a stone plunking in water, and you could say 'Paul.' " "I just can't live with Mark today. It's reminding me of ink blots, scratches, graffiti, too harsh." "Do you think anybody would think of toilet paper if we named him Scott?" "Zoe is nice, but people won't know whether it's one syllable or two. Besides, she would be too noticeable. It sticks out like a sore thumb." "Or big toe/toey." "That's not funny." "Cleo's a good enough name, strange enough, but it's beginning to sound like a puppet to me, like, if the shoemaker hadn't had Pinocchio, he would have had Cleo, you know?"

Renee and I were really communicating during that eighth month. We were downright gossipy into the ninth. For the first time I thought about Renee's name. I knew it was French. I asked someone who knew French better than I did. He told me it meant "reborn." What a beautiful name for my wife. She gets a second chance to be named, forever a second chance, I thought. I envied her. I didn't want to think about my own name too long. Jules. There ought to be a law.

Two weeks before the birth we decided on two names. Ian for a boy, Anneke for a girl. It made me want to have twins, just so we could have both names. I was drunk with the power of all this christening. I've always hated the empirical, the either/or in the world. I've always been both/and.

Ian was nice. It didn't rhyme with anything, it was too short to shorten, it would be hard to nickname. Anneke was equally good, and we could live with her peer group eventually tagging her Ann or Annie or Nikki. Still, I worried a little. Names beginning with vowels were always hard to write, especially as capital letters. Would Ian write his name like a telephone pole I or like a sail boat? Would Anneke do an A-frame, a big apple, or a crossbar A? I realized that I wrote the J in my name somewhere between the sailboat I and the big apple A. It made me a little self-conscious. I worried. I had nothing else to do.

Suddenly there was nothing left to say between Renee and me. We had these two names like Christmas lights to pin on a tree that wasn't there yet. We waited, and the waiting was worse than the eventual labor. Waiting out the last two weeks of a pregnancy is like waiting out unwanted guests. You yawn, you stretch and squirm, you don't talk, you don't put on music, you can't put away dishes. You look, you just sit there and look, like zombies.

After all our planning. All our careful planning. The birth was blue, soft, unspeakably peaceful, a bond somehow stronger than any marriage vows Renee and I might have stuttered by rote like morons. The baby was a boy, and he got himself an "Ian" as soon as the eyes had opened. We were being such good parents, letting him out like that. He sucked enough for Renee to feel like the concession stand at a ball game. He cried so little that I would pinch his bottom sometimes to see if he was still human. We were being such good parents.

Where did we go wrong? After the initial shock my parents realized his name wasn't "Eon" or "Ean" but "Ian." They were still saying "I an", the pronoun and the indefinite article, six months after the birth, but that was okay. Where did we go wrong?

A few years back there was a pop song called "The Name Game." Subconsciously, I swear it, instinctively (?), Renee and I began to sing that tune as we played with our baby. Ian go be-an, banna banna go be-an, Ian. It ran through our hearts and minds and slanderous tongues. Ian became "Go Beans" and "Mr. Go Beans" and (shudder) just plain "Beanies." I wonder if one day, grown up and living in Boston, suffering from too much flatulence in a tall and dangling body, he will ever forgive us?

Number One and Number Two

*O*NE month away from delivery. Jackie walks quickie-toed around the apartment like a mailman, all her letters in her belly. She's reciting different names to herself, trying them out on her unconscious. You'd think she was packing to take a trip, the way those names scurry through the air from the living room to the kitchen. Our cats hear her coming and scatter.

Me, I'm immobile. I haven't surfaced for eight months, obsessed as I am with the most important question facing new parents: What to call "number one" and "number two." I envision the fetus inside Jackie holding up one finger or two. Is that really number one or are you just pointing? Is that really number two or victory or peace or a two-spade bid? Sign language has its limits. I've got to be ready when the time comes. I am aware of the consequences if I'm not.

I read somewhere about one of our soldiers who was taken prisoner in the Korean War. He was tortured. They cut his fingers off. He didn't speak a word of Korean, so how was he to tell them he had to do number one or number two? Sometimes he just held it, whichever it was, and that was torture. Sometimes he just let go, from whichever end, and they punished him by torturing him some more.

Jackie says I'm going to get bone cancer if I don't move pretty soon. She's tired of dusting me each Friday, somewhere in between the floor lamp and the dining-room table. I'm afraid to move at this point. I might bump into one of those names she'd scattered everywhere in the apartment.

Jackie says I should do something constructive.

I tell her to bring me the dictionary. That would be constructive. I start with the *A*s and go to the *Z*s, looking for real-word synonyms for number one and number two. I know that babies learn to count on *Sesame Street* before they learn to rhyme with Big Bird and play with words. But they can't keep counting all their lives. People won't understand. Like the North Koreans.

When I was growing up, we used the translations of French-Canadian words. The penis was *oiseau* or *bird*. I laugh now every time I see Big Bird. Number two was *os* or *bone* and number one was *tinkle*. I never knew the French word for that one. My first crisis came on my very first day in first grade. I told the nun I had to tinkle. She told me to stop saying silly things and go back to my reader. I told her again. She said she would slap me if I didn't shut up. I shut up and tinkled on the floor. Why didn't you tell me? she asked in anger as she wiped the floor. I had to stay an hour after school as punishment.

Why don't you sit down for a minute? I ask Jackie. Too much to do, she says. I hear *too* in the dining room, *do* in the kitchen, and cats scattering like pool balls at the break.

Why don't you move for a change? Jackie asks me. I'm thinking, I say. When do you go to the bathroom? she asks. I never see you move. You must get awfully constipated just sitting there. I wonder about that myself.

At one extreme the dictionary gives me *urination* and *defecation* or *urine* and *feces*. These won't do. Nobody ever heard a two-year-old child say: "I have to defecate." At the other extreme there's *ka ka* and *wee wee* or *poop* and *pee*. These won't do either. Whoever heard of an adult saying: "Excuse me, but I have to go ka ka now."

My friend Gerald called me from a bar. I had Jackie bring the phone to me. Want to have a few belts? Gerald asks. No, I'm still trying to think up alternatives to number one and number two, I say. How about *beer* for number one and *beer nuts* for number two, Gerald asks. I hang up.

Mrs. Jackson, who works outside our back door in the garden every day, suggested that number one could be *wisteria* and number two *begonia*. Her son, who is an unpublished poet, offered *pools* and *stools*. A pornographic novel I just read used the words *whizz* and *cream*. I wonder how people can be so unhelpful and still sleep at night.

You've got to move, Jackie says. It's a week away from the due date, and she's obsessed with cleaning house. I can't. You've got to. There's a stain under your feet. It wasn't me, I plead with her, it wasn't me. It must have been the cats. I haven't seen the cats for weeks, she says. I can believe her. Even now I can hear them scattering.

Listen, Jackie, I initiate. What do you do when you go to the bathroom? What do you mean, "what do I do?" I mean, if someone asked you, what would you say? How do you call it? What? She's getting angry. You know, I say, number one and number two. I don't call it anything, she says. I just do it. And you're a dumb booger for asking.

We've been calling each other booger and turkey throughout the pregnancy. "How was your day, booger?" "Fine, turkey."

It's two days before the due date, and Jackie has begun moaning during the day. She used to moan just in her sleep. I wish I could help her. She says she wishes I could help her. She has installed an intercom system so we can talk without my having to move. She says she never suspected I would sit here rooted like some tree the whole nine months. She says she'll never have another baby with me, booger. She says that from her end. Even though she's nowhere in sight, the cats hear her voice and scatter. They can't stand all those names.

I've finished the dictionary. It's the most boring book I've ever read. No wonder you never see one in the doctors' offices. I think the words *liquid, gas,* and *solid* pretty much say it all for the excretory system, but they're a little vague, a little formal.

Jackie called the doctor yesterday. While she had the nurse on the phone, she told her all about me not moving for nine months. She put her end of the intercom next to the phone on RECEIVING and let me talk to the nurse. I asked the nurse about number one and two. You've regressed pretty far there, she says to me. I ask her again. Well, how about *US* for *uno* and *BM* for *dos,* she replies. I don't like abbreviations, I tell her. They can always be made longer. I shut off my end of the intercom and think of USA and IBM.

Jackie gave birth to a baby girl today. I watched the whole thing on closed-circuit television. I'm not sure which was more miraculous, the birth or the TV showing it all so I wouldn't have to budge.

I call Jackie on the phone. How was your day, booger? You know how it was, turkey. Her voice is very loving. So is mine, I think. So do the cats. They're swooning and doing number one on my shoes.

"Have you decided on a name, Jackie?"

"Yes. Gloria."

"Gloria? Who's that after?"

"*In excelsis Deo.* Have you decided on your names?"

"Yes I have."

"Well?"

"Booger and turkey."

"Which is which?"

"We'll let Gloria decide."

We live happily ever after, of course. Gloria and I are learning to crawl together.

The Holiday Inn Marauders

"WHERE'S the nearest restaurant?"

"Oh, about nine miles down the road. Take you, oh, two hours to get there. By mule team."

The hirsute desk clerk with the hawk's nose and the grubby little bellboy with too much starch in his cheeks, in harmony:

"Surprise!"

The man and woman, childless, obviously second-honeymooners of a sort, deflate like limp balloons. Stutterbox George, bow tie crammed like a doorjam to his neck, and the Neanderthal Wanda, hot bellows where a mouth should be, penny loafers tapping panic on the linoleum tile. This is a second honeymoon? Both look bewiffled at the camera, front and center, tongues wagging like old mufflers, eyes abounce.

Friendly. The friendly green and orange spire of a Holiday Inn, seen from an approaching station wagon, American-make, middle sixties, cameras mounted on the hood. Filters accentuate the green and orange. Warm colors. Watermelon colors. Very friendly.

Cut to George and Wanda, elbows askance on a restaurant table, pie-eyed and blister-faced from their partner push-ups on a Serta-tee family "deluxe." Rogue-rash of smiles on consummated faces, American-make, vintage fifties. Thoughts of haunched pillows back in the room. Taunts of a midnight dip skinny-style in the hotel pool after supper.

The Boy arrives. A frivolous flake in a velour vest, choirboy cheeks, angling a sizzling sirloin back and forth in George's face. George, by decree:

"Now that's a steak!"

Very friendly. Freeze frame. The H.I. logo. Subtitled.

HOLIDAY INN, WHERE THE BEST SURPRISE
IS NO SURPRISE.

Boy, have we got a surprise for them. The VW van
pulls in, the tires sprouting bulbs like corns on tired feet.
The Supper Express unloads its cargo: me and Zoe, the
sextuplets. We had waited six years to have a baby, then
had six with a flourish. Fainting, floundering bank ac-
counts, appeals to the usual charities. Free diaper service
from an anonymous donor. Royalties from newspaper
and television interviews. No, no fertility drugs. Just the
usual wonderwhack in the sheets, only without protec-
tion. Ask for one and we got six. Sextuplets. Ironic name
for it, no?

Democratic to the core, we had three of each sex.
There's Glen, Ken, and Len. There's Gwen, Jen and
Nguyen. Got the idea for that last one from a tour of
duty in Vietnam. Needless to say, Zoe's milk ran dry in
the first three days.

We managed. I get bonuses in triplicate. Good
publicity for the firm. More royalties from periodic fol-
low-ups in the newspapers and on TV. Clothes from the
United Fund. Three area colleges donating scholarships
for all the schooling, each one hoping to get all six to
enroll after high school. Only food remains a problem.
We've solved that problem with the VW van and the several hundred Holiday Inns around the country. Free food
for all children under seven. They're all six now. We go
out to eat every night. A salad and iced tea for Zoe and
me, full course "children's portions" for the Army.

They look like a police line-up going in the green
and orange and very friendly doors. Glen, who still picks
his nose in public, despite our best efforts to convince
him that this is antisocial behavior in the extreme. "I want
to be a person," he screams. Who can argue with that?
Ken, who has a similar pick-tic, in the vicinity of the
crotch. "If you'd get me bigger pants, I wouldn't itch so
much," he says. I get an economic itch in the back pants

pocket, just looking at him. Let him pick, limber up the fingers. Maybe he'll play concert piano someday. Len, the one whose name we always forget, because there is nothing abnormal to make him memorable. You gotta watch his kind, I keep reminding Zoe. He'll bring us woe someday. He'll bring us wheelbarrows of woe. Gwen, the precocious one. Keeps asking Zoe when she can begin wearing a training bra. Says we should send her off to a private girls' school, the finishing kind, so she won't be so corrupted by her "immature" and "little" brothers. We keep reminding her that her brothers all emerged before she did. "Really, Father." She calls us "Father" and "Mother." "You needn't be so vulgar." Her brothers ask her what *vulgar* means. She can't be bothered to explain. Jen, Jenny, Jennifern, so named because of her determined habit of eating shrubs. She wallows in the winter, putting on pounds as easily as Zoe puts on lipstick in the spring. It's better than eating bugs, I tell Zoe. But they spray everything with pesticides these days, Zoe counters. Maybe we can train her to eat just weeds, I suggest, and hire her out to rich people's gardeners.

"Why did I marry you?"

Zoe asks me this question three or ten times a day. It varies with the weather and the children's school year. When they're on summer vacation, Zoe is too tired to ask.

And Nguyen, my favorite. How could I forget? She reminds the others at least as often as Zoe asks me her predictable question that she's "daddy's little girl." "That's disgusting," Gwen says. I think it's rather nice. I've already decided to bequeath all my worldly possessions to Nguyen when I go to my Maker, who, by the way, only mustered one.

The hostess pretends not to see us. She plays with her ring, looks at her watch, shares nervous glances with the cook. We're used to this hopeless hesitation. You should have seen the hostesses when the kids were three.

"Yes, sir?"

"Eight, please."

"Yes, sir. I'll have to look. You understand. Maybe in the back room . . ."

She exits, her feet backpedaling like a centipede. She takes her time. I'm sure she's gone out the back door to have a smoke. She comes back with a monotone.

"This way, please."

We're ushered in to a very back room. Any more steps and we would be in the coffee shop. We can hear guests splashing in the pool behind the prefab walls.

"On vacation?"

I wonder why they always bother to make small talk, trying to delay the inevitable extra waitress and strained cook, the inevitable frenzied serving and cleaning up. She has the look of someone who has arrived late at a welfare line.

"No, just out for supper."

"So you're not staying with us?"

"No, just driving by. We saw the friendly green and orange, you know. Thought we'd stop in for a 'bite.' "

A bite? she's surely thinking to herself. Call that caravan of starving lookalikes a bite? Free food is bad enough, but the thought of serving nomads must rankle her self-esteem just a little. She tries to coax our crowd with long smiles and musical suggestions.

"My, you children are pretty. I bet you're hungry, huh? Well, we have a 'special' that I just bet you'd like. Hamburgers and french fries, and all the Cokes you can drink. Would you like that?"

"We'd like to see the menu first," Gwen says from the shoulders, with just a smidgeon of pomp to her very prepubescent whine.

"Of course, honey. Of course."

The hostess, surprised at so much caveat emptor in a little girl, lets her prior "waitress voice" from truck stops and diners come puttering through. "Honey." They always call you "honey" in such places.

What we don't know, but of course we suspect it,

is that we're famous in all the Holiday Inns around the country. They talk about us at their executive conventions. How to stop all this free food every night, how to keep "good help" from quitting when they see us coming, how to turn an admittedly unhealthy situation into profitable promotion for the H.I. empire. Once they called up photographers after we'd ordered. They planned to use the photos and film in their national TV ads. The friendly green and orange spire, close-ups of our entire family, a soothing narrator suggesting that, if the Sizemore sextuplets think Holiday Inn is a "super" place, then shouldn't everybody in America be going there? It was a complete disaster. Gwen told the interviewer that her body would probably never blossom properly from so much "cardboard" food. Glen picked his nose, as usual. Ken stirred soggy french fries in his Coke. To our surprise, even quiet Lenny had something to say. "When you've seen one of these joints, you've seen 'em all." They never tried again.

Why me? this hostess must have been asking herself, all that time by herself in the back room. Why me? the cook must have been asking, overcooking someone else's food. Why us? the other eaters must have been thinking. We just want a clean and well-lit place. A quiet meal. A cheap price. No surprises. Why us?

Little do any of them suspect that they will have to wait to be served, wait for their coffee, wait for their checks, because the Sizemore sextuplets never, I repeat never, order the "special." They want to be persons, each little stomach with a mind of its own. They will order six different dishes, six different drinks, six different desserts. And they'd better have as many flavors of ice cream as Howard Johnson's, or we'll be complaining, at the top of our sixteen collective lungs. Make that fourteen. Zoe's too tired to say anything.

"Why did I marry you?"

She's not as tired as I thought. The waitress needs four pages on her pad to get all the orders. Glen wants steak, medium-rare, mashed potatoes, plenty of ketchup, Coke, chocolate-almond ice cream. Ken wants fried chicken, french fries with tartar sauce, Sprite, strawberry shortcake, with one scoop of vanilla and one scoop of chocolate on top. Gwen wants the chef salad, skipping the cheese and egg slices (she's watching her diet), un-sweetened lemonade, no dessert. Jen wants clams, a couple scallops substituted for her potato, melted butter to dip them in, 7-Up but no ice, chocolate cake with one scoop of peach ice cream. Nguyen really wants hot dogs, but she orders tossed salad, French dressing ("Why do they call it French, Daddy?"), and iced tea, with three slices of lemon, "just like her daddy has . . ." Who am I leaving out? Oh, yes, little Leonard. Len orders the "special" to choruses of hoots and boos from the others.

The waitress repeats what she's written.

"No ice," Jen reminds her.

"Yes, ma'am."

I watch my growing boys and girls gobble up their food with knives and forks and fingerfuls. I watch napkin after napkin, smeared with ketchup or melted butter, being wadded up and cast aside. I stare proudly at chicken bones, half-eaten hamburger buns, melted ice cubes, knowing that once again I have provided for my family. Once again we have not gone hungry. I intend to ask the travel agent if Holiday Inns in other countries offer the same freebies for the under-sevens. I intend to tell Zoe that we'll have to go soon, wherever it is we want to go, before next year.

Zoe chain-smokes Camels, tapping her broken fingernails on the table, looking up and down both rows of chewing, sipping, gurgling, grunting open mouths and filled stomachs. I eat slowly, leisurely, chewing my time as well as my iceberg green under French orange. Friendly. I'm almost glad to be a father, wondering why I agonized so much before we had kids.

"Why did I marry you?"

Zoe exhales Camel smoke in my face. She looks very

romantic in this off-color smoke. I know she's happy, every last chewed fingernail of her is happy, even though she asks. I continue to savor my salad. I have the right to savor what I'm paying for. It's an American and unalienable right. Very American. I bet they don't have sextuplets in starving India, forgodsakes. It's the U.S. of A., I say. Very friendly. Even if I do have to leave a fifty-cent tip for something that's free.

Microwave ovens and fetal monitors, all in a free market society. Whoppers, Whalers, Sirloiners, Kentucky Fried, Egg McMuffins, epidurals. Green walls and orange lights for those faces of fear. Erased pain and induced labor. Pills to not get kids, pills to get kids. Pills to forget kids. Fast-food feelings. Green and orange and redwhite-'n'-blue. And very very friendly. Shell is a gas, Joy is a detergent, and Mayflower will always be a moving company.

Canada Dry

BARRY and Eunice are two of my closest friends. He's a Unitarian minister and she's a part-time carpenter. He's in charge of the "Rap with God" series at the church, and he also organizes the Friday night mixers for divorced, separated, and single people. She used to play golf a lot before they got married. Apparently she could have gone on the professional tour, she was that good. Now she swings a hammer in her spare time. I have mentioned these things about Barry and Eunice in order to round them out, so to speak. But these details about them are very insignificant and need not concern us here. I want instead to talk about their problem.

Their problem is that they want children. They have always wanted children, and it is only in the last year or so that they've told other people about this formerly private wish. They've gone public with their problem. At first Eunice agonized in private, going secretly to doctors, other ministers, palm readers, old farmers' almanacs. She took fertility drugs without telling Barry. She was willing to risk the possibility of sextuplets. Anything was better than nothing.

Meanwhile Barry prayed a lot on his own. The "Rap with God" series tackled the biblical message of "increase and multiply" with suspicious frequency. Barry got superstitious and carried rabbits' feet around. Certain days on the calendar were marked off as magic in his mind. He read up on the occult in the public library when Eunice thought he was out buying groceries. He too went to doctors, who prescribed everything from Gregorian chants to ginseng bubble baths. Nothing worked.

They got together on their problem before they went public. It had to be one thing or the other. They weren't communicating, because they couldn't think of anything else. They began to joke about how it was possible for Abraham and Sarah, in their ripe and gay nineties, to have a child born unto them, compliments of the Lord. Such jokes were very short-lived. They began to go to doctors together.

They found out that Barry had a defunct (undropped) left testicle, which took the magic chromosomes out of any sperm he concocted. Even with an operation the situation could not be corrected. So the alternatives were clear. Barry and Eunice could live their lives out, waiting for a miracle in their nineties. They could adopt. Eunice could try her luck temporarily outside the marital state. Or they could artificially inseminate. They decided upon the last alternative.

I have no idea what they must have gone through to carry out their intentions. All I know is that it's not as easy to get artificially inseminated as one might think. Barry and Eunice found out after much asking around that there were only two doctors in the whole city of Philadelphia that did artificial insemination and that they were specialists who did nothing else. These doctors are not allowed to advertise, so the Yellow Pages weren't much help. Word-of-mouth from other doctors was the only way to get to these two. For the sake of fiction (and to avoid any reverse malpractice suits), let us call them Drs. Smith and Mallory.

I suggested to Barry that he should be happy at least that there wasn't a monopoly in the field. He said that Smith and Mallory had never formally met, but that they, of course, knew of each other, even referred the most difficult cases one to the other, in the spirit of free enterprise and friendly competition. Besides, if one could stick the other with a well-nigh impossible case, it might drive the other out of business. As I said before, friendly competition.

I was part of one visit to Mallory with Eunice, the very first visit actually, when Barry was unavoidably detained with prior commitments at the church. Mallory just naturally assumed that I was the husband, even though Eunice spoke of her husband's problem in the third person. And we didn't bother to set him straight. I don't know why. Usually you refer to a doctor by his title and leave off the last name, but for some reason Mallory was just plain Mallory to me from the start. Perhaps it was because he was one of a rare breed of two. I hope that it wasn't subconsciously due to any feeling on my part that he wasn't really a doctor, a normal doctor, and so should go by his last name. In passing I allow that possibility.

Mallory was immediately affable, charming, even delightfully childish with us on first meeting. His bedside manner allowed him to meet us at the door. There was no receptionist in the outer office. The wallpaper in the outer office looked like that in a children's nursery. The walls were filled with row after row of modestly framed photographs of smiling babies, proof to anyone who cared to look that Mallory was indeed successful at his chosen trade.

He had an enormous mood ring on his fourth finger that lit up red like a flare when he shook my hand. I wondered if he himself was married and whether or not his ring still shone stars and stripes when he touched his wife. As Eunice explained her husband's problem, Mallory smiled affectionately at me, almost paternally, not without pathos. I kept thinking about those rows and rows of smiling babies in the outer room, framed for posterity, and every single one of them smiling from ear to pudgy ear. I kept thinking and wondering as Eunice went on talking.

When Mallory began talking, he told us that all women could be separated into two camps: the wets and the drys. He said that Eunice could be considered Dry, but that she needn't necessarily remain that way. With a grand flourish of his right arm he alluded to all those baby photos in the outer room. It wasn't the money, he insisted, that kept him in the field, although both he and

Smith came very high indeed. No, it was the satisfaction he got from helping God and the couple fulfill a master plan of procreation. He spoke to us for three hours, and never once did he mention the word *artificial* in all that time. He preferred to think of what he did as "extended intercourse." He was very proud of his sperm bank, which he kept in cold storage. We would, of course, be able to inspect the bank, if we decided to go through with this extended intercourse. Mallory went so far as to say that being a doctor wasn't enough in his line of work. One had to be a good banker too. I could see his mood ring light up as he talked long and lovingly of being a banker. He was as reliable as MasterCard, he said.

All of the semen samples in his cold-storage vault were of the highest quality, he insisted. They kept complete dossiers on the males from whom these samples had been extracted. Not a genetic deficient in the whole bunch, he insisted. These anonymous "donors" had undergone thorough physicals, all free of charge of course. They had been well paid for their semen, Mallory said, and he lamented that the cost had to be passed on to the customer. No, it was not the money. He waved again to the outer room, and I half expected the babies in those frames to take a collective bow. Mallory insisted upon an eight-by-ten photo of the baby once the pregnancy had come successfully to term. This, too, was at the customer's expense.

Mallory said that God had blessed him with a success rate of almost 99 percent. It made me think of Ivory Soap to hear him talk, such a high percentage of pure. Mallory said that I should not feel left out or in any way replaced, since the resultant child need never know about the extended intercourse. He was, of course, sworn to secrecy in such matters. For that very reason he could not give us the names of any of his satisfied customers.

I felt like playing the devil's advocate, despite Eunice's disapproving stares. I asked Mallory if Smith would give out any names.

"Smith, Smith, he's a bungler. An amateur. A Victorian butcher, if you ask my opinion. The man has no sense of artistry. To him, all medicine is artificial. Kidney transplants, pacemakers, insemination, they're all the same to him. All artificial, if you should ask him."

That ugly word had finally surfaced. The mood ring vibrated purple on his fourth finger. I had never expected such a timid dig to produce a near stroke. Mallory ignored me during the rest of the conversation.

He showed us his guns. Not just a doctor and banker, Mallory was also a collector of the rarest squirt guns ever known to man. His collection numbered almost seventy-five guns, from glass to plastic and other synthetics. If Eunice decided to go through with it, she and he would choose the one gun best suited to her pelvis and vaginal opening.

"Do not let the shape or size of these guns frighten you, madam. When the time comes, I assure you that I will be quick and sure. And I must emphasize that you will not feel a thing, not the least discomfort. Some women have complained of a mild tickle, but never anything beyond that. And with local lubricants, even the tickle can be avoided."

It was all so arrogant, his guarantees of success, his victory over the common tickle, his mood ring for motherhood. It was all so antiseptic, so predictable, so Sani-Flushed. I began to envy the discomfort of couples driven to the backseats of cars, the panic in the knees at missed periods, the utter surprise of sex with all its unpredictable potential for disease and conception. I wondered what happened to couples who came to people like Smith and Mallory and had babies put in like they would have tonsils taken out. I wondered if later in life they would suffer from some neurosis unchronicled by the AMA. Guns, hidden banks of test-tube semen as potent as the nerve gas stored by the army, and those rows and rows of grateful babies. It all seemed so bizarre to me. And yet so natural too.

Eunice would have one week to think it over. If she decided to go ahead, she was to come back at the end of the week for a thorough physical, at which time she and Mallory would devise their "game plan," as he called it. The game plan consisted of maps and charts, choosing the kind of sperm, the days of the month best suited to her bloodstream and ovulation, the physical positions most advantageous to her particular pelvis, the very gun they would use. They could even decide upon the frame for the baby picture, I thought.

I consoled a nervous Eunice on the way back to the church by telling her that I had been the third of seven children, but that my parents, too, had had trouble conceiving. They had gone through four years and thirteen doctors before they found out that my mother had a kind of natural birth control, an acid deposit that was not harmful to her but which killed my father's sperm before they could do their duty. This acid deposit could be removed, and it would grow back naturally. But after four years of waiting they had accumulated enough anxiety for a lifetime. They had it removed seven times, and seven times the magic wand sparkled with success. It was the first time I had ever told anyone this story. I don't think Eunice heard a word I said.

Barry and I went out for a beer that night to discuss the matter man to man. He said that Eunice was convinced. And was I? I didn't know, I said. It wasn't me who was in the middle of this extended intercourse. I asked him if he didn't somehow feel that Eunice would be having an affair with an anonymous donor, and that Mallory was, as middleman, a kind of pimp. He said he did feel a little jealous, but what else could he do? Eunice had looked so beautiful in the car driving home, just thinking about conception, that I had felt some physical attraction for her. I was tempted to offer myself to Barry as a surrogate. At least he knew me. He knew what he would be getting. I resisted the temptation.

"It's such an unexplored area, you know? I mean,

we know it happens every day with animals. New life in test tubes. And you read about it from time to time, how they're ready for humans. But is it natural? I mean, what does God think about all this? I feel a little like Eunie and I are in the middle of some Boris Karloff film. And all those men who donated, I mean, why would they do it? It can't be just for the money. I mean, that would be the ultimate prostitution, wouldn't it? But what must they feel? Do they get a zap in the spinal cord in their airplanes or on their construction jobs or even on the golf course when their semen clicks with Eunie's eggs? And this Mallory, he's human, isn't he? How can he be sure, with all those test tubes and all those guns? He must make a mistake here and there, no? And what must be going on in his head, to be in on it at the conception stage instead of at the delivery stage, where doctors are supposed to be?"

Barry agonized and did all the talking. I listened and drank all the beer. I felt elated after all. I was in on a pregnancy scare, and I had never unzipped my pants. It was enough to make one believe in the Virgin Mary, the Immaculate Conception, and all those other unexplained miracles in the days before artificial insemination. It used to be a joke in our family that my father had had seven children in order to prove how potent he was. How would Barry accept all the playful handshakes and knowing winks of men who would see him as more than just a man of the cloth? And what if Mallory weren't able to achieve instant bingo with Eunice? Barry and Eunice had not even admitted this possibility. And how could they, if they were to go through with this ordeal? They had to have complete trust. It was as though they were dealing with the divine. Only the divine wore a mood ring on his fourth finger, and the sudden mention of the name *Smith* could cause thunderstorms in this celestial realm.

In the week that followed, I didn't see or hear from Barry and Eunice, but I knew that they were going to go ahead with Mallory and his mandrakes. I felt happy for them but somehow ill-at-ease inside my stomach. I could not for the life of me remember Mallory the man, although I could picture every inch of baby fat on the cheeks of at least a dozen of Mallory's gallery. Baby after baby, I thought of them, I dreamed them, I felt like talking to them. I was running a kind of invisible kindergarten in my mind all week long.

Another week passed, and I knew that Eunice must have picked her semen, picked her position, picked her day and hour and gun. Being that definitive about something like conception must have changed her perceptions about everything else in the world, from her sense of the morning alarm clock to her sense of the end of the world. I waited for them to call me. I respected their privacy, but still I felt a little left out. After all, even Mallory had mistaken me for the helpless husband on that first visit. And if by chance I were to see him on the subway someday five years from now, was I supposed to hand him a cigar, ask him how business was, talk about preschooling for my test-tube toddler?

Another week passed, and I could no longer stand the suspense. I called. Barry answered, and his voice and vocabulary were the same, but the tone had changed. It was rambling, no longer phlegmatic, doing the rhumba. His voice bubbled up at the ends of sentences, as though they were commas for an auctioneer. He didn't say a word about the two weeks of silence. He talked as though we had just seen each other that very day.

"Eunie's on fire, I tell you. Went out yesterday with the clubs. Shot a forty-two on the front nine over at Whitemarsh. Been pounding away with her hammer too. She's already got a baby rocking chair made. You should see it. You give it a little push and it just swings and swings, like some little guy was in it."

"Any word yet?"

"Not yet. But she's been shot up five times. We'll know soon. It's bound to happen. Bound to. She's on fire, I tell you."

With promises to see each other soon, I hung up. I kept thinking of Eunice burning, her adrenaline having been transformed into lighter fluid. I thought of Joan of Arc and no children.

I began to wonder in the weeks that followed what the interest rates were at Mallory's sperm bank. I began to have fantasies about Eunice getting all incinerated over what could very well have been tubes of sugar water or squid ink or something. What if Mallory were just planting the seed in her mind and not in her womb? They would still have to pay, and Mallory could send her to Smith as one of those "difficult" cases. I wondered if Mallory took off the mood ring when he washed his hands of something.

My own mother has gone through a couple of hysterical pregnancies, when a television show about children or a random baby carriage in the street set her off. Or when one of her daughters-in-law would announce a pregnancy. My mother would miss one or two periods, the doctor would inspect her acid deposit, would hold his glasses in his hand and calmly ask her what she thought she was doing, and at her age. And maybe, just maybe, her doctor talked her out of it, before her idea took shape. I have always trusted in her extra sense about children. She had to have the doctor for the acid deposit. But had she never had a doctor, she might have had twenty children. I'm sure she must have thought about it.

In the middle of the night it hit me. I went through bouts with the cold sweats until morning, just waiting for the banks to open. I realized why I remembered those babies' faces so well. They all had the smug and smiling stamp of Mallory on their faces. Of course. In a field as restricted as his, what was to prevent such a case of megalomania? All Mallory had to do was to juggle several dossiers. After all, how many dossiers would an eager customer wish to see? Three or four? He probably did get donations from that many males, so that these few dossiers, at least, would be legitimate. But what about the rest? I could see him ejaculating in tube after tube the wet squeeze of his own semen. I could see him smiling into his bathroom mirror at night, while he brushed his teeth, knowing that he was fathering, not families, but entire cities. No wonder he waved his arms so proudly at all those faces on the outer-room wall. They were probably his kids, every last one of them. The thought of Eunice giving birth to a little Mallory made me shudder. I resolved to see Smith, to confront him with it.

"How did you find me?"

"I asked my doctor, Doctor. He didn't want to tell me. He had to do some asking himself. But I've referred several people to him. He owes me, if you know what I mean. He told me about you and Mallory. All I needed was an address."

"I see. So. What can I do for you?"

"It's about Mallory."

I explained my fears. I told him about that first visit with Eunice, without telling him Eunice's name, or my real name for that matter. I told him about the rows of baby pictures in the outer room. I felt I could tell him, since there wasn't a photo in sight in his office. There were only cheap watercolors of sanitary landscapes, brooding dogs, juggling clowns. I told him about the sperm bank. He said that he, himself, had no semen on reserve, and that his patients had to wait for donors on a customer-by-customer basis. It reminded me of those open-air seafood restaurants where the customer could point the accusing finger of final judgment on some squirming live lobster, and an hour or so later, he could shell and eat his cooked victim. I told Smith about the guns. Smith only had one gun, the standard issue from Upjohn Pharmaceuticals. I told Smith about the mood ring. Smith wore a plain wedding band. The more I told him, the more I wondered why I wasn't telling the police, and what was someone as unremarkable as Smith doing in this business? And finally I told him about my fears of a Dr. Frankenstein, of a megalomania unparalleled in this society since the concentration camps.

"But you have no proof, my dear fellow."

"Proof? What proof? I want to know if you think it's possible."

"Unlikely. Mallory is in good standing with his profession. We both are. No, it's very unlikely. It's more likely that this whole tale tells us more about you than about my competitor. You're unmarried, are you not? And you've been emotionally involved with your friends from the beginning, perhaps even more involved than you care to admit with the wife of your friend. Perhaps you even wish, no doubt subconsciously, so you needn't deny it, that you were going to be the surrogate father."

"But why are you defending him? He's your rival, isn't he? It *is* possible, isn't it? I mean, the dossiers, all he'd have to do is juggle the facts on a few dossiers."

"Supposing your hypothesis is correct. I'm humoring you, mind you, I don't really believe there's the slightest thread of truth in anything you say. But just supposing. Those dossiers are confidential. They could never be used in court, and even if they could, no real names are used on them. That's to protect the identities of our donors. You can see why they would wish to remain anonymous, can't you? And any resemblance you might detect in those baby pictures, well, anyone knows that we see what we want to see in baby faces. They are so malleable, you see."

"I see."

"You see what?"

"I see you're in cahoots together. Birds of a feather and all that."

"Please, my good man. I'm sure you mean well or you wouldn't have come. But think of your friends. If they are successful in having a child after all this time, do you think they really care who the donor was? Even if everything you say is true, do you think your friends would be appreciative of your zeal? Do you think they would help you take this thing to the top, as you put it?"

"Thanks for your time, Smith."

"Wait a minute. You got your doctor to refer you to me. I haven't even asked his name. I'm sure you wouldn't tell me if I asked. But let me in turn refer you to a doctor I know who would be most happy to hear you out."

"Thanks just the same."

I am not well, it is true. But not for the reasons suggested by Smith. What I had thought to be an isolated case of mass patrimony could very well be a national conspiracy with a tacit understanding to keep silent on the part of all these practitioners of extended intercourse. The old live-and-let-live philosophy.

I am not well, because I have to live with these awful truths. Barry and Eunice are deliriously happy. One of Mallory's shots has found its mark, and Eunice has stopped playing golf again. Barry wants me to be there for the birth. He says that he gets confused, whether to thank God or Mallory or me. He says I've been a kind of doctor to them, a kind of husband by proxy to Eunice, a kind of child to them both. I don't understand this last remark. I certainly don't want to be adopted by them. I have this awful truth to tell them, and I cannot tell it. What if Eunice had a miscarriage? What if Barry had a nervous breakdown? What if they both never wanted to speak to me again? But then, what shall I do? How shall I hold their newborn baby? And when they send me their announcement picture, how will I help but see the two of them, with the blissful smile of the newly married on their faces, holding an undergrown Mallory on their laps?

I have begun seeing a doctor who refuses to listen to me talk about all this. He seems to have all the time in the world to listen to me, however, and he asks me to tell him everything I can remember from my past, everything and anything that comes to mind, no matter how insignificant. It's all the same to him.

I can remember that my mother used to talk French with my grandmother when they didn't want any of us children to understand what they were saying. I remember that my grandmother had moved her whole family to Michigan from Montreal when my mother was still a little girl. I remember that every one of us took French in high school, long after my grandmother had died. I don't remember why any of us took French, since there was never any chance to use it. My mother stopped speaking French the day my grandmother died.

I remember that she and my grandmother used to say *"aller au Canada"* a lot in their conversations. *Oh, Bernice, elle est allée au Canada. Arlette, est-elle allée au Canada? Oui, Gertrude est allée au Canada.* We didn't need to wait for high school French to know that *"aller au Canada"* meant "go to Canada." We always thought it strange that they should speak in French so that we couldn't understand, when all they were saying was that so-and-so had gone to Canada. And with all that talk of Canada you'd think the two of them would have gotten homesick. But neither of them ever went back to Canada. And none of my brothers and sisters ever went either.

I spent two years in France when I was a student, and I don't know why. At least, I don't remember. I know that I majored in French in college, which was unusual for a man to do in those days. I knew at the time that this language proficiency would be of no use to me in getting a job. Maybe I spent those two years in France just to justify my inevitable unemployment after graduation. I got along pretty well when I was over there. I asked my mother one time in a letter if she thought I should have gone to Canada instead. She didn't answer in her next letter, so I wrote her back and asked her what going to Canada had meant when she and my grandmother said it. In a P.S. to the next letter I received, she told me that it was just their way of saying someone had gotten pregnant and dropped out of sight. In those days you couldn't say someone was pregnant, not even in French, not even in front of seven little children who wouldn't have understood anyway.

My doctor thinks we are doing fine. He's even excited about the baby. He knows what I mean when I say that Eunie has gone to Canada wet.

Circles

I am not a morning person. I always write at night. I never revise, for fear of killing my characters or finding out something about myself. I certainly never reread what I have written the morning after.

I awoke at 5:10 this morning, awoke from a dream in which I was thinking and speaking in Spanish. I had just taken the cure from a Gypsy sorceress, a Sephardic Jew, and I was trying to get back to my *colegio mayor*. I couldn't remember the name, so the cabdriver was going around in circles, his meter ticking pesetas like the metronome atop a piano, ticking to punish my memory. I remembered the name of my *colegio mayor* as soon as I woke up: Marqués de Enseñada. How could I have forgotten? He was a big name during the Inquisition. It's said he had a special talent for wrenching confessions from Jewish women.

I awoke to a morning of blue and purple, that magic moment when night slips off a negligee and rubs thighs with day, a morning of blue and purple not unlike those mornings Joyce and I used to wait for, dancing in the nude to low-playing jazz, low so other people wouldn't wake up and find out we hadn't slept, dancing so we wouldn't have to face making love, because that might cause us to sleep.

Joyce is a real woman. Joyce is her real name, although she has many others. Joyce is the first woman I loved enough to want to be a woman myself, to know what it was like to receive my boil-festered tongue with the texture of frog bodies in those blue and purple mornings of all-night dancing in the nude. Joyce really wore a purple scarf around her left wrist, because she said a piece of clothing always made sex more erotic. She was right. I've never known another woman to wear a purple scarf like that, to dab the scarf in the wet of her genitals at the height of the dancing when the trumpet took off on its own, to dab the scarf and run it under my nose and over my lips, still dancing, freezing the moment in my memory. I've forgotten many women since, women with whom I was much less reticent, women with whom it was all over but the sleeping before the change of body polarities at midnight. I think it's because Joyce knew how to make love to my sense of smell. The erotic for me is synonymous with the unique.

Joyce is an imaginary woman who's loved so many men since loving me. It doesn't matter. I still love her and she still loves me. Our circles have expanded, but we haven't stepped outside of each other. Joyce is also a writer, a better writer than me, which complicated our knowing each other but which completes the circle of our memory. I have never known memory to be anything but circles. So everyone reappears sooner or later, especially loves lost. Those reappearances have something to do with modern physics, the sound waves of a locomotive loudest as the train approaches, because the waves are shorter, softest as it leaves you behind, because the waves get longer. So too memory elongates. Like an earthworm after rain, it stretches out to copulate.

Joyce had a theory of circles. She would meet at least five new people in a day and mentally draw a circle around herself and the new person. When love was lost but still itching like a forgotten birthdate in the mind, she would lay the person out, the prelude to burial. She would step outside the imaginary circle and put an X through it. It was her way of divorcing. She never believed in an afterlife.

I've read somewhere that the circle with an X inside was one of the markings used on Jews in the concentration camps. I have no way of verifying this. Joyce is a real woman who's divorced in New York City. Her husband didn't want any children. He was Jewish too. With me she had a circle. They're harder to abort.

So Joyce is a real woman I still love, now through fiction more than in life. There are other real people in this story. And there are the required faces of fiction. The meeting of the two makes the circle more complete than we could ever have had it in real life, if real has any meaning left. The Inquisition went a long way toward putting an X in everything.

"Sha, Ian. Eat. You're supposed to."

"I'm waiting for Elijah."

"Maybe you have to eat and trust, Ian. Have faith that he'll come."

"But his wine will spoil, Daddy."

"It's just wine, Ian. It's a symbol. Joyce, help?"

"I'll try. You know when Daddy takes you to church and he gets communion?"

"Yes?"

"Well, Daddy believes that God comes in the communion. You don't see anybody in the bread, do you? But Daddy believes he's there. Just so. You may not be able to see Elijah when he comes unless you believe he's coming."

"Is that right, Daddy?"

"Yes. Now hush. Let Mommy say the prayers."

"Grampa Abe says the man should say the prayers."

"Yes, well . . . Mommy knows them better than I do."

"Because you're Catholic?"

"I guess so. Anyway, it's time to be Jewish now."

"I get confused."

"Ian, be Eliezer."

Bill and Joyce left Madison with bloodshot eyes. They had spent the night at John Van's apartment as usual. John Van had played basketball until ten o'clock the previous evening. He had come home and had gone to bed. Bill and Joyce counted on his exhaustion and early sleep. Downstairs they played jazz records, ate strawberries, drank wine, and talked. Touched. The talking had become a kind of touching.

They would take the plane from Madison Airport at ten o'clock and be in Fairfield, Connecticut, by one. The previous weekend they had gone to visit Bill's parents in northern Michigan. This weekend they would visit her parents. It was a joke for both of them. They had gone to Bill's parents and had escaped without insult or intimidation. His parents had suspected nothing. They had listened attentively while Joyce tried to explain why she wanted to become a rabbi. Now they were going to Fairfield, and Bill thought he should be making up some story to tell her parents, the reasons why he wanted to become . . . a priest? The rabbi and priest would put them off the track, would make them accept this couple as the close friendship of opposites, not the sensual stuttering trumpets of soft jazz, not the talking through touching as the blind sometimes touch each other's mouths to give physical birth to words. They were clearly nervous. They talked about John Van in order not to talk about themselves. John Van, the bean-sprout man, the frustrated jock in the always unwashed T-shirt, the eternal bachelor with the buck-toothed smile, forever the victim of disastrous blind dates arranged by people like Bill and Joyce who loved him so much that they would subject the various "blind" women to dates with him, dates that more often than not consisted of lifting weights or jogging in the gym, dates on which an unusually high number of women came out of the closet and declared themselves lesbians.

Talking about John Van had become a code, a secretly comfortable conversation sprinkled with in-jokes, pseudonyms, and made-up words. They were clearly nervous. The only alternative to talking was touching. It took a lot of touching to board the plane.

"Fairfield. It sounds like the Elysian Fields. Do a lot of Jews live there?"

"Don't worry, Billy. You'll be fine."

"Tell me about your parents. What are their names? What are they like?"

"Daddy's Abraham. Twenty years with Westinghouse. He'll probably take an instant disliking to you. He always does. It's okay, Billy. You're not Jewish, and you're not a potential doctor or lawyer. So you're not potential, that's all. He knows you're a writer too. Wasted, like me."

"That's succinct enough. Your mother?"

"You'll love Mommy. She's gorgeous, really gorgeous. Once Janie and I asked about sex. Mommy decided she and Daddy should show us rather than tell us. So they ran around naked for two weeks. No more questions. Nice, huh? And once this man named Saul came to dinner. He loved Mommy very much. At the end of the meal he apologized, and then he asked Mommy to go away with him. My father asked him to leave. Mommy cried. She's beautiful and warm and kind. There's the hug of the world in her hugs."

"What's her name?"

"Risa."

"Beautiful name. Know what it means in Spanish?"

"What?"

"Laughter. Risa is laughter."

"So that's what a trill sounds like. You have to teach me Spanish. I could learn. I already know a couple words. Ready?"

"Ready."

"Buenos Aires, nocharena."

I was standing there in Madison Airport, holding Joyce loosely in my arms. She was laughing, but it was crying. I was silent, but it was crying. John Van stood a few feet behind her, bloodshot and slouching, muttering asides to himself about "young lovers."

"Why are you leaving like this?"

"Please, Joyce, it'll only be a year. We need the time. We need to know through time."

"Hell we do."

"Besides, if we can show our parents we still want to be together after a year apart, what can they do?"

"Disown us, kill us, same as now."

With promises to write every day, we separated. I could feel the blood sink in me to a freeze, my forehead giddy, my knees wanting to urinate. I sat down so hard in my seat that the seat flopped back. I would be in Madrid in the morning.

"Why are you leaving like this?"

"I have to know. I have to go to know."

I knew it was a mistake as soon as I boarded the plane. There are times and places that we know instinctively to be wrong, fundamentally wrong for our bodies. I knew some of these places by their names, without ever having to go: Dallas, Texas; Chicago, Illinois; DaNang, Vietnam; Australia; Germany. I had to go to Madrid to know it was wrong from the very first day.

I sat in an aisle seat, crying now that Joyce couldn't see me. Next to me in the middle seat was a dark-haired secretary from Cleveland with big pouting lips and very fleshy calves. Her trip to Spain was being paid for by her boss, a skinny young Jewish executive who sat near the window shuffling his thumbs, a habit he probably picked up while dictating memos to this secretary. In the morning I would wake up with the secretary's head on my shoulder, her pouting lips sending low moans up to my cheeks.

"Why are you leaving like this?"

"I don't know."

"I wish to God you had given me a baby first."

John Van had driven her back to Madison. I learned much later that he had told her I was a fool to leave her and that she would be much better off forgetting me. I think she tried. Her first letters were half *X*s and half *O*s, side by side to signify that we were together, even though apart. The next step would be to join them.

"If we had a son, what would we name him?"

"Ian is a good name."

"Ian it is. That means John, St. John. Baptism by water?"

"For you, Billy, water is most important. For me, blood. That makes Ian, not John."

"And if it's a girl, what? Risa?"

"No."

"What's the matter?"

"To name her Risa would mean an early death for Mommy."

"Maybe Sonrisa, then. That's Spanish for *smile*."

A test. Bill is graduating from the University of Wisconsin and going to Madrid for a year on a Fulbright-Hays award. The month is May, the air is wet and windy, time slows down in the open windows and the smells of green shrubs rising from the ground to the lights and the wine inside the room. The staffs from both the male and female sides of the dorm have gathered together for good-byes. Joyce is there. They dance. It is the first time they have ever touched in a year of knowing each other, a year of reading each other's writing, a year of sharing each other's passions for other people. The music is loud and full of clichés, but it is slow enough and full of weight, the weight of their bodies that touch, fit each other snugly, especially at the thighs. The thighs stiffen as they rub together. Their pliant bellies give way to each other, undulating like warm bread dough flattens as it falls against the hands that beat it. Their bodies sweat beneath the clothes. They say nothing. Bill can smell the wine on Joyce's breath in her hair and around her ears. He knows that if they were to pull their cheeks apart, there would immediately be a coming together at the lips. John Van circulates between the dancing couples, the emcee of the dance. The two walkie-talkies of the staff don't seem to be working tonight, folks, he says to Bill and Joyce. When the music stops, Joyce smiles and goes back to her room, leaving Bill with a giddy twitching in the tongue, the sensation of being unable to sleep, the time of talking to oneself in the fold of the pillow that smells like wine.

A test.

"Why did you and Mommy get married?"
"So we could have you."
"Mommy?"
"So you could have us."
"Did you know I would be a boy?"
"We knew you'd be an angelface. That's all that mattered."
"Do you have to get married to have a baby?"
"No, but other people like it better if you're married."
"What other people?"
"Well . . . like Grampa Abe, for instance. Why are you asking all these questions?"
"I need to know. I'm sure I want to have babies, but I don't think I want to get married."
"You'll be married one day. Patience, Ian, it all comes."
"Mommy?"
"Yes?"
"Do you think Gramma Risa knows about me?"
"She knows. More than we'll ever know she knows."

A test. Bill comes to see Joyce for the weekend. Immediately he invites her to spend the next weekend with him at his parents' cottage in northern Michigan. She accepts. She begins to brood, to contradict whatever Bill says, to deny his every kiss with a turned cheek and bowed head. Take me home, she says when they've just arrived at John Van's party. Tell me something about Spanish literature, she insists as soon as they've gotten in the door of her apartment. Find me some lox and bagels, she urges at three in the morning, even though she knows he can't stomach Jewish food. It takes two hours to find an all-night delicatessen fifteen miles away. I'm not in the mood, she says to his approaching face. Much later she would tell him that three different men had tried to sleep with her that week. He leaves her with his shirt still unwrinkled on Sunday morning.

"Do you still want me to come to your cottage?"
"Yes."

A test.

"Joyce, Madrid calling. Merry Christmas. Happy Chanukah."
"Billy?"
"*Te quiero*. I love you."
"Billy, shut up and listen. I want to tell you something."
". . ."
"Billy?"
"What's happened?"
"Mommy's dying. She's got cancer and she's dying."
"Joyce, I'm sorry."
"Sorry? God. She's dying."
"What more can I do, ten thousand miles away?"
"I can't talk anymore. I've got to catch a plane."
"Sir, your three . . ."
"It's done, operator. She's not there anymore. She just never hung up."

A test.

———————

"Billy, look. That's my bicycle over there."

"I didn't know you had a bike."

"Of course I do. It was stolen. There it is, I tell you. Will you help me get it back?"

"It would help if we had a car. Let's walk back and get it."

"No, no. It might not be here when we get back. Let's take it now."

"But it's got a lock. I'll have to carry the damn thing."

"Do you want to help me or not?"

Two months later, when he'd gone to Spain, she would write and tell him that it wasn't her bike. That she didn't even know how to ride a bike.

A test.

"Did you know I would be a boy?"

"We knew you'd be an angelface. That's all that mattered."

Joyce used to call me angelface.

A test.

"Joyce, what's the matter? Why haven't you written?"

"I've been very busy. The story's going to be published."

"That's great news."

"No thanks to you. Too Jewish, he says. Narrators should be objective, he says. Shouldn't talk like the people talk in the dialogue, he says. A lot you know."

"I never said I knew it all. Besides, you asked me."

"I changed the ending too."

"Why?"

"I don't know."

"Whatever that means. Listen, did you get my letter?"

"Which one? They're all the same. Listen, Billy,
things change. You keep bringing up last summer, playing remember when. You tell me to say this or that to
John Van. He doesn't even remember anymore."

"I'm s—"

"You can't freeze people. Can't bottle time."

"Okay, let's skip it. We can talk about all this in a
letter. Listen, how's your mother?"

"Have you read my daughter's stuff?"

"Yes, sir."

"So?"

"Well, I'm not an expert, but I'd say she's good.
She's very good."

"She tells me you write too."

"Yes, sir."

"Who's better?"

"I don't know about that. I guess I wouldn't com-
pare us."

"Daddy . . ."

"You know any writers who are millionaires?"

"Daddy . . ."

"An interrupter. I got an interrupter for a daughter.
Joyce, for God's sake, don't paw the boy. He's old enough
to answer for himself."

Blessed. With two syllables. He was blessed. Ian was
born with his hands folded, his little fingers encircling
each other like the links on a chain. He was born with his
brown eyes wide open, the eyes of the wise man who
looks like he's asking questions, even though he already
knows the answers. The *havdaleh* candle came in his eyes,
burning because they never blinked. The eyes to make
grown-ups shiver, because they never blinked. He was
born with his little legs wiggling, as though he thought
he could swim through the air. But his head was com-

posed and firm and on his neck. His mouth was open, ready to pronounce. But his bulging brown eyes still asked the questions. They were enormous, the reflection under invisible glass. And bloodshot like a boil.

I fell in love with her at first sight. She smiled when I came in. Smiled without getting up. She smiled and the little wrinkle marks around the corners of her mouth were like quotation marks. Even when she joked, I couldn't laugh fully, because the joke was also for learning. She could see my confusion. Joyce looked nothing like her. After all the hugging in the doorway, all four of them turned and looked at me. Joyce got her bird's body from her father, her slightly irregular teeth from her father, her nose from her father. The father was quick with his handshake, quick to give, and still quicker to withdraw. His hands were clammy. His eyes never blinked, and when he smiled, quickly, as though he shouldn't be smiling, his nose looked like it hooked over his upper lip. An eagle, I thought. Janie was tall and full of warm colors, her body rippled with soft, suggestive curves. But she spoke loudly and abruptly like her father, as if she were afraid that she wouldn't get her sentence finished before an interruption. When I responded to something she'd said, she would look off, as though distracted, and follow my sentence with her own previous sentence repeated, as though she were erasing my sentence, as though I had never spoken. Joyce played quick repartee with her sister and father, defending me against attacks I wasn't even aware of, couched as they were in sprinkled Yiddish. Meanwhile the mother bathed me in light, hallowing the mud on my shoes with her rainbow eyes and her benumbing smile. She asked me nothing. She carried the family quotation marks around her lips that smiled without interrupting the one-liners of the others. Her smile. Sonrisa.

I got off the plane in Madrid and helped the secretary and her boss from Cleveland find a hotel. Speaking

Spanish for them was an attempt to justify the mistake of my being there. The sun was hot in Madrid. My genitals stuck to my legs when I walked. I wanted to bow my brain as I bowed my legs, to keep myself clear from chafing. I fell asleep talking to myself. In the morning my hips were full of pain. I thought it was from sitting seven hours on the plane. In the mirror I saw the strawberry patch of boils that has been with me ever since.

I stir myself like soup, stewing in my own juices, knowing I'm guilty of something, not knowing what, looking, finding not the sin but the punishment for the sin, the festering like lava that spurts before the full eruption of catharsis. I close my eyes, still looking. A watched boil never pops.

Boils were one of the nine plagues visited upon the Egyptians. Like a pregnancy, I thought. I've got eight months to go.

A test. God threw everything he had at Job, destroying his cattle and sons, killing off his wives, sending the tempters to ease Job into doubting. God poked Job with his testing, laying on his massive hands. And everywhere the stigmata went along the folds of Job's skin, boils popped out like yokes from an egg. Job looked like a frog. Still, he never questioned. He just smiled, his graying teeth like weathered grave markers. Patient Job. He was rewarded thousandfold.

St. John was the favorite apostle. He always sat on the right hand. Gentle John, whose eyes never blinked. But before he could be hallowed, he had to be boiled alive.

There is no cure for cancer.

A test.

"Mommy, does it hurt? Are you suffering?"

"Only when I laugh."

The laughter was the cure. The cure that came too late. That waited years to come. And only came from her, so the living could go on.

"Mommy, it's fun to talk to you when Dad's not here."

"Ian. Such a thing to say."

"Know why?"

"Why?"

"Because I feel I've known you longer. Did I say something bad?"

"Hush."

"Why are you crying?"

"I'm not . . . crying. Dripping is all. I'm a sponge. You're a rum cake full of treats. Me, I'm a sponge cake."

"Know what else?"

"Tell."

"I love you."

"Have you decided on a name?"

"What name did you pick, Dad?"

"Anthony."

"What's he famous for?"

"Finding things you've lost. He's the patron saint of memory."

"I think I'll take Christopher."

This was the day before Ian's confirmation.

I was away when she died. Had I been there, I couldn't have said anything. We never said anything to each other. We understood all there was to know from the very first look. Had I been there, she would have smiled at me, knowing what plagues were in store for me. I would have forced a smile myself, and with that smile, the others would have hated me forever. Joyce never understood why I kept quiet, because our love was based on talking that was touching. I was away, so there was no possibility of touching. Had I been there, I would have embodied silence. Mark was there with Joyce, listening to her rages against God, her denials of mortality, her bile to the absence of an afterlife. She married him before the death. To everyone else he was the saint who endured her madness. To me he was a martyr. He refused to have children, even when she was full with the beginnings of one. She divorced him.

"Billy, you know what I hate most about the Catholic Church?"
"What?"
"They deny that I even exist. If you marry a Protestant, you can't divorce her without committing a sin. If you marry me, you can annul in a second according to the Church. Pagans don't count. It's like the damn Arabs. Three times and out, woman."

I was born in late August, between Leo and Virgo. Joyce was born in early July. Ian was born a few days later. Obviously Ian belongs to Joyce. There is no cure for Cancer, the cardinal sign of water.

"For you, Billy, the water is most important. For me, blood."

In the ninth month of my year in Spain, Abe gathered together his closest relatives and friends, numbering one dozen, to say kaddish and sit around a circular table, their eyes on their hands in their laps. A week later they would sit shiva and mourn around that empty table.

A year later they would unveil, shagging their nets around a tombstone. These rituals are provided so that one need never think in the midst of grief, a grief that shakes the body from the head to the toes, preventing thought.

These prayers were not for Risa.

In the ninth month of my year in Spain I found Magdalena Ofarim, the Sephardic sorceress. I found her in an alley in the center of Madrid, her star of David at the end of three spiraling alleyways. I expected crystal balls and moth-eaten curtains, a thousand rings on gnarled fingers. Instead I found an old woman, plump in her stomach, as though she had been sitting all her life, continually about to give birth. She was sitting when I entered, she was sitting when I left. I never saw her legs. She walked with her fingers over my skin. The fingers felt their way along the flesh, as though she were shuffling cards. Hers was not the human touch, warm and coarse, commingling with my touch. Hers was the touch of insects, cold and probing, without feelings or hesitations, making me itch wherever she touched. I tried to tell her about my boils in Spanish. She shook her head and smiled. I had to take off my pants, to bare my whole lower body before the benevolent eyes and the plant-stem hands. Wherever she touched, boils popped. I was bleeding and dripping a belt of bruised cherries around my naked waist. I had come for the cure in the middle of the night. And she had clapped her hands to make them warm, rolled up her sleeves, and put her gnarled stumps against my raw buttocks. In the depths of her throat there was singing, the low drone of many voices behind closed church doors to someone who stands out in the street. When a boil popped, she would clear her throat, the doors would open, and it was clear that absolutely no one was inside.

"You know, Billy, I couldn't hold out. I started sleeping with people soon after you left. Maybe I thought it was silly to be so old and so innocent. Maybe I was trying to hurt my father. I don't know. I was promiscuous in a strange sort of way."

"I want you to know, Billy, that I was faithful to you to the bitter end. Till Grand Central. Terminal points."

I believed her both.

Boils and carbuncles are due to inactivity of the skin, to bad blood from putrefaction in the system, to constipation. Boils are an instant sign that the body is full of poisons and in a low state of resistance.

Some of the minute glands die; sometimes the root of a hair dies; a little pimple appears, which, if treated immediately, soon disappears. The red spot is followed by tenderness and great pain. The bowels must be kept open when one is afflicted with boils.

Eating a dozen or so oranges a day is recommended.

High enemas are recommended.

A poultice of white fluffy bread or a potato poultice covered with cloth or lemon and garlic tied to the boils all are recommended for overnight cures of boils.

If one cannot translate these into Spanish, then prayers are recommended. Especially the kaddish, about the ninth month.

There is a good deal of wishful thinking in writing a short story like this. The more one feels desire, the closer one gets to writing a novel. I feel I have failed, and I need to say so before the story ends. I wanted to write a story about Joyce, and I've failed. I keep wishing for a photograph, the perfect portrait for all poses, and be done with it. She resists. Because it is not her story. Nor mine.

I fell in love with Joyce because she was a boy, someone who hid her body in order to compete with men. She had never stopped dreaming the little girl's dreams, the dreams that only boys are expected to fulfill.

She was fulfilling. She was every insult I had ever heard, hurled with reckless abandon at a tow-truck world. Who do you think you are, you crummy schmuck of rubber mud, she would say without thinking. Her compliments came in hyperbole spoonfuls that had to do with food. You're rich as rum cake, you scrumptious supper strudel. You knew when she liked you. It was baked beans and pork if she didn't. I have missed all that in the story.

I was totally unprepared for purple scarves about a wrist, for off-key Jewish humming jazz, pretending she was black and full of torches, for eyes that said make love to me, thick and cozy as cat's paws. To compete with her carpenter's saw of a tongue, I used to kid her about wearing a training bra. I was totally unprepared for the breasts that spread out like braided bread and the nipples as big as campaign buttons. All the things she got by her mother she kept hidden under clothes. I have not been able to describe them here.

Fiction cannot comprehend the whippoorwills of open mouths for feedings in the mornings with Joyce. It would sound too perverse, as though I were describing five-year-olds making love. Fiction is equipped for describing the death of love, not the day-long mornings, with tiny cobwebs in her slanted eyes, her whispering I'm hungry like a command. It would sound too much like nursery rhymes.

A photograph is what I needed. I have always liked the jargon of photography, because it is so buried in the terms of time. I asked a friend of mine to help me reproduce some photos. He said that we would sacrifice a lot of clarity, because we were already a generation removed. I believe him to be literally correct.

Magdalena Ofarim had cured him of his boils. He had new legs to stand upon and then suddenly he had nowhere to go. Joyce had stopped writing. So he went to France and Denmark, every country hosted by a woman, the women to whom he told this story, changing her name to Risa. They took him in and held him close, but they did not believe him.

Then a letter came, inviting him to meet her in New York. He left Madrid before the height of the bullfighting season, before the summer sales on suede coats and classical guitars, before the swarms of tourists at the Prado. He slept and flew home in the morning.

Joyce graduated with honors and went home to her mother who was dying of cancer. She went home decided. She would not marry Bill. That for her father. She would marry someone else, someone Jewish and very quickly. That before her mother . . . She kept Bill waiting a week in New York, waiting and afflicted with new boils. She met him at Grand Central, telling him he hadn't changed. He slapped her face. The red spot was followed by tenderness and great pain.

"What is Passover, Mommy?"

"It's the freedom of the Jews, their finally going home."

"Daddy?"

"It's the swallowed-up Egyptians beneath the Red Sea."

"There must be as many people as there are fish in that sea, huh?"

"Hush, Ian. We've got some questions for you to answer."

Dear Billy:

It's been five years now. And it's Yom Kippur. I'm sorry for everything I did to you. I'm sorrier for everything I didn't do.

Love,

Joyce

After great pain a formal feeling comes. It is the substitute for laughter, to keep the living in their skin.

After death there are only simple sentences, facts devoid of feelings, words shorn of their power to mean anything but what they say they mean. The child's question alone is loaded with innuendo, with the wisdom that needn't ask a question. There is nothing more similar than the purple light about a window when a baby is born and that same unpaintable light about a bed when a mother leaves off hearing those she's borne and begins to converse with the other side. Both are freeing in the end. And the love of a man and woman, from whatever faith they espouse and reject, is ultimately as unstable and as nil, as *nada* as boiling water when compared to the love between a mother who died too soon and a son who was never born.

The Ninth Month

*E*IGHTH month. Moira is obsessed with dying. On the verge of giving birth, she is reading *On Death and Dying,* she is dreaming her grandfather's death over and over, each night more painful than the last, trying desperately to let him go. She has never forgiven him for abandoning her, for dying and allowing his survivors to cut down the oak tree in front of the old house in north Georgia where they used to take walks together every night after supper. It was a magic tree, and it became a photograph of him for her when he died.

She ponders her own death. She cries when she thinks of the child she carries inside, the dependency on her life for its own like an anchor around her waist. She feels like sinking each time she stands.

She asks me why I didn't go to my grandmother's funeral. How did I deal with my grief? Where did it go? Why haven't we talked of this before? I have never seen my mother cry at a funeral, I tell her. This is no answer, Moira says.

I remember the last two years of my grandmother's life only through what my brothers and sisters have told me. I can only guess at her sudden senility, her submission to a bedpan at night, her gradual sinking to a crouch when she walked. I imagine those endless stories she used to retell my mother when my mother would be trying to do the cooking or sewing or ironing. My mother would tell her that she had heard them before. My grandmother would continue, driven by the sheer impulse to talk. Ten minutes after she had finished a story, she would retell it: how she met my grandfather at a square dance, how the wheel on their buggy broke on the way home, how her parents waited up the whole night with a shotgun. Often she would change the details of the stories. Her father would be waiting up with a whip instead of a shotgun. My mother would stop what she was doing and scream. It isn't true. It isn't true. My mother was going slowly insane.

I remember the last year of my grandmother's life only through what my mother has told me. My mother cried when she told me of her visits to the home where my grandmother had to be tied to the bed, where she refused to eat, and where they inserted catheter tubes and intravenous feeding tubes. My grandmother cried like a young girl to be exposed this way, her legs arched in the air and fastened to stirrups, as if she were giving birth. She begged my mother to untie her. She begged for the letting go.

My last physical memory of my grandmother was of a smiling, carnivorous woman, who played cards like a man and who told salty stories to distract her opponents and make them play the wrong card. I didn't want to let go of that memory.

This is no answer, Moira says. She speaks of the Carlos Castaneda books, in which Don Juan tells Carlos that he must make friends with his death, that death must become his ally in order that life can be lived without fear or attachment. Carlos resisted and had to take drugs to let go.

I can only think of a section from Peter Handke's *A Sorrow Beyond Dreams,* in which the protagonist-narrator (Handke himself) describes his mother's suicide and the numbness he feels at her funeral. He speaks of having read somewhere about the surprisingly high number of people who have contracted fatal diseases while attending funerals.

I used to be an altar boy at funerals. I used to make the incense that the priest would shake over the open casket. I remember the Dies Irae being played on the organ, how peaceful it must have been to be dead to that music. All of these faces that I never saw in life. I met them with their hands folded in stiff repose. I watched their relatives file out of church, sobbing and yelling. I stood by the priest while he said the last prayers to the casket descending. Gravediggers yawned to the side, waiting to cover the ground again. I never cried at these funerals. I just stood there, wondering whether or not these dead people got to carry their last thoughts with them.

I remember my friend Terry's death in the second grade. He was hit by a car while riding his bicycle. Our whole class knelt around his open casket and said the rosary for his soul. I couldn't think about his soul. I was too distracted by the red hair. Terry had blond hair, but his head wounds had been so severe that they had dyed his hair red. I was the altar boy at his funeral too. Two days later my grandmother told me that she had been the midwife at Terry's birth. She didn't go to his funeral.

For some time now I have been dreaming my own death. More precisely I have been dreaming the pain of dying. At the point in the dreams when I am to die, the exact point, I disappear and our baby is born.

Sixth month. Moira has urged me to read the books on childbirth for several months. I am too distracted to get beyond ten pages at a time. Finally, however, I have read one. I am especially intrigued by a section on crib deaths. It is the shortest section in the book, but to me it is also the most poetic. The writer speculates that crib deaths are still a mystery to the medical profession because they haven't considered the psychological and emotional attachment between a child and his mother. He says that leaving a child alone for many hours at a time or with an unfamiliar baby-sitter for an entire evening may be one cause of crib deaths. I am fascinated by the ability in such young infants to let go of life, especially when my parents have told me how desperately my grandmother clung to life. Is suicide the only way of letting go for adults who have forgotten what they knew instinctively as children?

Fourth month. Moira has read that it is now possible to determine not only the sex of the unborn baby but also its exact shape, size, and position in the womb through the use of an ultrasonic scanner, which bounces sound waves off the fetus, producing its contours on a graph. She wants to know if I would like to know all these things ahead of time. I think about all the dreams I have had about the baby being born blind. I have always been afraid of losing my eyes, and now I have apparently projected that fear onto our unborn baby. Yes, I would like to know. No, I tell Moira, I'm content to wait and see. She sits in my lap and hugs me. I have said the right thing.

Fourth month. In a dream I remember when Larry and I were attacked by some high school seniors at a seventh-grade dance. We should have run away from them, but we have stayed to fight. I am pinned by one boy and hit by another, while Larry fights with their leader. Suddenly it is they who run away. Their leader has knocked Larry's glass eye out in the snow. They are terrified. They think it is his real eye. Three hours later they turn themselves in to the police. It is the last time Larry and I do anything together. I am terrified too.

Fifth month. Our friend Michelle has gotten a job in the Midwest and is leaving us. I can see the tears behind the thick glasses. I hug her and kiss her good-bye. I laugh and say that it feels good to be able to hug a woman firmly from top to bottom, so good I had almost forgotten. Moira smiles politely. She tells me later that she is hurt and jealous. Neither of us is prepared for this jealousy, because Moira has never been possessive. Perhaps it is hormonal. I have read somewhere that the writer Strindberg once told the painter Edvard Munch, himself obsessed with jealousy, that jealousy is not the fear of losing someone, but rather the fear of sharing. I worry about sharing Moira with our unborn baby. Still inside her womb, it is, nevertheless, the magnet that sucks up all our physical senses. It is the only topic of conversation we have left.

Fifth month. I dream that I am dying in the Middle Ages. Our baby is summoned to be my doctor. I am surprised to see that our baby is a boy. He prescribes bloodletting. I hemorrhage and die.

Fourteenth month. I am aware of sexual feelings toward my son. My sexual feelings for Moira have not decreased, but these feelings are different from those I feel for Seth. I take off Seth's wet diapers and marvel at the involuntary twitching of his beautiful body. Just as breast-feeding is Moira's special time alone with Seth, so too this ritual with the diapers is mine.

I stretch the foreskin of his penis and feel no guilt. There is only pleasure, a joy as simple and unexpected as finding something one thought was lost forever. I fold his buttocks in the flat palm of my hand, making a swing of my hand to rock his lower body back and forth. We stare at each other, and he smiles his toothless gummy grin between two dimples. When I am changing his diapers, I feel no need to talk. I feel only this deep unspoken language of the skin, father rubbing son, son swinging with father, trust and unspeakable joy. I realize that sex and excrement are inextricably joined in these plump folds of skin.

I feel somehow homosexual and realize that this is the first time that I have ever felt the word instead of intellectualizing it. I have always been able to picture two women lying together, talking as well as touching, knowing exactly how to give pleasure to one another, because it is the same as giving pleasure to oneself. I have never been able to visualize two men lying together.

Often when Moira and I are walking somewhere, commenting on the people who pass by, I have said something like: "If I were a woman, I could really go for him." In order to verbalize I felt constrained to provide a heterosexual context. I now suspect that "if I were a woman" was really a mask, a useless condition of saying "I could really go for him." I remember, too, Moira telling me once that the only men who had ever treated her as a person, and not as a sex object, had been homosexuals.

Third month. Moira asks me what I am writing.

Eighth month. Moira is withdrawn, preoccupied with her own silence and the noises she alone hears inside. She has read that unborn babies are sensitive to light and sound. Each morning when I am getting dressed to go to work, she opens the curtains in front of our bed and lets the sunshine swim in upon her naked belly. It pours slowly, like beaten eggs. She has told me that she has spent entire days like this, watching the sun move microinch by microinch over her naked belly.

She listens to the groans inside and guesses that the vehement movements she's been feeling for several weeks are complete somersaults inside her womb. She sings the Protestant hymns her grandfather used to sing to her. Sometimes she is so withdrawn when I come home that I have to repeat a question several times. "How was your day?" I finally scream at her. She tells me that I must not speak above a whisper when I am this close to her. Then she returns to silence, her hands folded on the skin cushion created by her protruding belly. I have noticed that breasts seem to shrink when a woman is lying down. I am amazed that a pregnant belly is just as pregnant lying down as standing up.

Fifth month. Halfway through the pregnancy Moira is obsessed with death, with birth and death, with time. She says she sees the cold impersonal wings of enormous angels flap above her head, flap and curve in semicircles, giving her umbrellas in her eye of the storm. Everything is temporary, Moira says to me, sometimes three times a day. Everything is temporary.

Fifth month. Moira dreams that our baby will be a boy. She is told in the dream that the immediate past life of this baby was spent as a Buddhist monk, and that this monk knows nothing of Western culture. He is afraid to come to us. Moira meditates on this dream. She is told that all past lives in this baby's chain of being have been spent in the East and that this entity has attained a high degree of spiritual development. This will be the first life as an Occidental, and the purpose of this life will be to learn technology. Our baby will learn to live with machines, and I who know nothing about machines will be his teacher. The Buddhist monk moves his face back and forth, his mouth wide open. Either he is petrified or he is very hungry.

Fourteenth month. Seth has become very familiar with Moira's breasts now. He no longer closes his eyes and chokes on her milk in eager, almost pathetic gulps for survival. He is confident now. He keeps his eyes open, holds her breasts with his little fingers, cupping her breasts, the way a mother holds her baby in bathwater. He is easily distracted now, sucking for five minutes, looking off and laughing at the slightest sound, returning to sucking. He falls asleep at her breasts, and when she tries to withdraw them, he instinctively jumps to sucking again, the way seemingly subdued cats become rigid and pounce on a piece of string.

One habit has remained from his early days at the nipple. As she pulls him toward her breasts, he still rockets his head, his balloon cheeks, his wide-open mouth back and forth, back and forth, a rocking chair, a lullabye, as if teasing himself, savoring the milk to come. I have seen this movement of the mouth before somewhere. It was immediately familiar to me the first time Seth did it.

Third month. Moira asks me why I am writing.

Tenth month. Moira and I lie in bed, tired beyond sleep. Her breasts have been engorged for over a week. The rouge of little pink bruises remains on her breasts, from the engorgement or from a slight infection. I joke that we have a vampire on our hands.

She asks me to suck her milk, to relieve her pain. I am so tired from walking the baby after feedings, from burping him, from letting him cry his indigestion in my ears, that I hear her ask me as an echo. I feel too tired to comply, but I do. The milk is pleasant to my tongue, coming not in a rush, as I had expected, but slowly, imperceptibly, as if it were there all the time. It tasted like saliva after making love, saliva with the faint taste of peppermint.

Fourteenth month. Moira's episiotomy has been completely healed for some time now. We have resumed sexual relations. It feels awkward to say it that way. It makes us sound like two countries who have signed a new treaty. We have resumed diplomatic relations.

The desire I feel has been strong since the birth. I don't understand such desire. It is not like lust or desire from absence or abstinence. I'm not even sure it's entirely sexual. It's like finding something I thought I had lost forever.

It is also curiosity. I want to go in and see with my penis what our son saw for nine months.

Fifth month. Moira and I have stopped having sex. It is my fault. Recently, while having sex, Moira was perched on top of me. I could see our genitals rubbing. I could also see that each time I moved upward with my penis, something else would move in her lower abdomen. I imagined our baby coming out with a hole as big as a holster in its head. I imagined poking its eyes out. I cannot go in again until the baby comes out.

Tenth month. We have become shy with each other. We close the bathroom door behind us. We catch each other staring at each other. "I need to know, now more than ever, that I am your lover as well as your wife and Seth's mother," Moira tells me. I nod and look into her eyes. There is fright there, not fear, but fright, the way animals experience fright as the impetus to flight. Her eyes are asking me: "Who are you and why are you in bed with me?" Everything is temporary.

Tenth month. Moira and I spend much of our time in silence, listening to the sucking sounds Seth makes. He sounds like a frog to me, his *ribbet* and slurping, his baby wheeze of ecstasy. A photographer asks for a smile with the word *cheese*. I think of Seth's sucking as the word *galoshes*. He sloshes through puddles without worrying about splotches or laundry. I love to see his drunken face come whoozy-eyed off the breast, his eyes rolling, his lower lip unglued, his whole spine collapsing with the first burp.

Fourth month. How can you write at a time like this? Moira asks me.

Twelfth month. Moira writes in her diary. "I like to turn off the sound when looking at TV and watch the antics of people in the commercials, superimposing my imaginary dialogue on them, based on my own preconceptions. What foolish antics people cavort through when they are eavesdropped on by silence."

Fifth month. I do not understand such hatred. For five months now I have felt alone, living apart from Moira and our unborn baby. I cannot come to grips with this pregnancy. When I try to think about it, I get angry. I hate this child who has done nothing to me. I experience this pregnancy like a Robbe-Grillet novel, a labyrinth that keeps changing each time I try to go through. I hate this child for putting Moira's belly between us. We can't even have a decent hug anymore. I hate this child for my loss of privacy, my sense of losing my privacy. I hate this feeling that now Moira and I must really be married, because we are going to become a family. I hate this feeling that now I am expendable, because I have created a new generation. I can die now, because of this child. I hate, and this hatred is driving me insane. I drink coffee until I am dizzy and I hear babbling voices in my stomach. I smoke three packs of cigarettes a day. Nothing is as I had expected. I thought I would find Moira's bulging body attractive. It's like a statue, impregnable and asexual like a statue. I can't go on not telling Moira this. I must share this hatred before it devours me. I do not understand such hatred, unless it is the same thing as desire.

Thirteenth month. Moira writes in her diary: "Is a refusal to use words a fear of really discovering how things disappear when we examine them? Or do we use words out of fear of the same thing? What tremendous drive makes us want our children to develop language? What is it in the infant that infuses every sound with the potential for meaning?"

Seventh month. Moira has not written in her diary for seven months. She has read more than fifty books on childbirth, prenatal yoga, and child development. I have not read these books. What are you writing? she asks me.

Second month. We have decided to have a home birth.

Fourth month. I have read the chapter for fathers in one of the childbirth books. I have taken notes.

Say lots of love words during the birth.

Get cameras loaded and ready (fix loose leg of tripod).

Have washcloths and water basin.

Make orange-juice ice cubes.

Arrange comfortable chairs, robe, and slippers.

Buy wine, flowers. Cigars?

Take phone off hook.

Tell neighbors so they don't call police when they hear screams.

Remind Moira of enema before delivery.

Borrow extra pillows.

Hot water bottle.

Get heating pad, extra blankets (boil and sterilize same).

Remind Moira of closed eyes during first stage of labor.

Check insurance again.

Seventh month. We had dinner with our midwife. I have said very little, listening in awe to the quiet words of confidence between Moira and the midwife. How can two women who barely know each other be so immediately intimate with each other?

I am jealous of this easy smiling and whispered sharing between women. It must be very fulfilling to be a midwife. To be mother and doctor at the same time. To give birth and let another give birth.

Fifth month. I understand that this hatred I feel is the hatred not of losing someone I love but of not being able to share. I hate that I am not biologically able to give birth myself. I hate and that hatred is so much desire put on like extra pounds in the skin.

Fourth month. I have put on twenty pounds. Moira says that empathy is fine, but this is going too far. I can't help myself. I can't get to sleep at night. I walk and end up eating myself to sleep. I can't concentrate on my work. I have lengthened my lunch hours, because eating is the only period left in the day when I don't have to think.

Fourteenth month. I have just come back from a business trip to New York. I stayed in Manhattan with Marcie and her husband. Marcie had been a close friend of mine in graduate school. It was me she came to, five months after her boyfriend had joined the military, five months after she had had her last period. It was I who called the doctor, who took her to the doctor's office, who held her hand when she came out shaken with the confirmation of her pregnancy. I never told her that the doctor called me that night, asking me if I was the father. When I said no, he told me that I shouldn't have brought her myself, because now I would be liable if Marcie got any crazy notions about a paternity suit.

Second month. I asked my father what he felt during the months of his children's pregnancies. Joy, he said. I asked Matt, our neighbor, what he felt. Nothing, he said. I told John at work that I was having very strange dreams about becoming a father. He said I should see a psychiatrist. I called Marcie on the phone last night and told her I thought I might lose my mind before the nine months were up. She said I should keep a diary.

Fifth month. "What are you writing?"

Fourteenth month. I have completed Seth's baby book, including a family tree of photographs from both my family and Moira's. I feel such a physical sense of history looking at four sets of grandparents, imagining Seth's reactions years from now when he looks at them. I feel, too, such a sense of time in these pictures, time that is not chronological and so jumps out at me from the page. The picture of Moira's mother, for instance, is from last year, when she was fifty-nine. The picture of Moira's grandfather, which is underneath her mother's picture, was taken when he was forty. The father is younger than the daughter. My grandmother's picture was taken in 1949 when she was eighty-three. The adjoining picture of my grandfather, who hated to have his picture taken, was shot in 1880 when he was thirty. Could this thirty-year-old man with the piercing eyes of stern religion and the strong gnarled hands of the farmer have been married to this withered woman with the bifocals, sunken cheeks, and elfish grin? I think I understand how deep time runs in our skin through such pictures. Time and death. This tree is petrified.

Fifth month. I have a meditation in which I meet myself as an old man of eighty. He looks a little like my grandmother, except that his smile is vegetarian. There is a typewriter on the windowsill. The window extends from one wall to the other, and purple night is filled with shooting stars outside that window. He takes my hand and leads me to the window. We look down and there below us is the ocean whose waves are blue faces with white beards on them. I look at the old man, and he is smiling. He says that the wrinkles of the ocean that I love so much are the same as the wrinkles of age on his face and that I needn't fear growing old anymore. I tell him that I have always lived my life with the expectation of dying from a heart attack at fifty. He says I can still die at fifty, it doesn't matter to him, because he exists right now and will always be there. But I will have to survive in order to join him. I look at the typewriter. "What are you writing?" He says I will have to live to be eighty to find out.

Ninth month. After fourteen hours of heavy labor

with no medication, Moira gives birth to a baby boy. She announces to everyone there that his name is Seth.

First month. Moira tells me that we are pregnant. I hear her say "married" instead of "pregnant."

Fifth month. "What are you writing?"

Fourteenth month. I have completed Seth's baby book, and I realize that there is more here than just a family tree of photographs, more than this haphazard collection of strangers who all had to lie together to get Seth. I know that the secret of time that I, the old man of eighty, promised to teach when I got there is already in the ages and arrangement of these photographs, if I could only decipher them. I feel that there is a connection between these photographs and the collection of short stories that I have been writing for the last fourteen months. For the moment I only know that I have kept my sanity by allowing the expectant fathers in these stories to be insane. I look at little Seth and he looks at me. I am thankful that he has allowed me to experience homosexuality and incest as more than abstract and intellectual taboos. I watch his mouth move back and forth at Moira's breasts, and I think of a line from Roethke: "I tell time by how a body sways."

I realize that Moira's nine months of pregnancy were different from mine. My nine months began in her fifth month when I stopped trying to control our unforeseen dreams and gave in to chaos. My nine months have ended in this fourteenth month with the birth of my short-story collection. I understand the postpartum depression at the end of fiction as the cessation of desire, and I now know that one must learn to jump rope with time in order to have sex with desire itself. And when one can no longer feel even the memory of desire, there is no more rebirth.